BIRTHDAY BOY

DAVID BADDIEL

Illustrated by Jim Field

HarperCollins *Children's Books*

First published in Great Britain by
HarperCollins *Children's Books* in 2017
HarperCollins *Children's Books* is a division of HarperCollins*Publishers* Ltd,
HarperCollins Publishers
1 London Bridge Street
London SE1 9GF

The HarperCollins website address is:
www.harpercollins.co.uk

7

ISBN 978–0–00–820051–0

Printed and bound by CPI Group (UK) Ltd, Croydon, CR0 4YY

To Grandpa Colin

PART 1
FOR HE'S A JOLLY GOOD FELLOW . . .

CHAPTER 1
BIRTHDAY BOY

S am Green was really, really looking forward to his eleventh birthday.

I mean: *really*. He couldn't wait. In the days leading up to it – his birthday was on the eighth of

September – he simply wouldn't talk about anything else.

"Have you sorted your school bag, Sam?" his mother, Vicky, would say in the morning.

"I'm thinking an *Adventure Time* cake this year, Mum," Sam would reply. "With Finn, Jake and Ice King figures. What do you think?"

"I think you should get your school bag sorted," she'd answer.

"Do you want to play football?" his friends would say to him at break-time.

"What about a magic party?" he would reply. "You all come, having learnt a different magic trick, right, and then we each perform it in turn – me last, of course – and then . . . where are you going?"

"To play football," they'd answer. "Break's nearly over."

"What would you like for dinner?" his dad, Charlie,

would say to him and his younger sister, Ruby, in the evening.

Ruby would open her mouth and say:

"Actually" – she said "actually" a lot – "I fancy shep—" but before she got any further Sam would be saying:

"I'd like a telescope. And a skateboard. And new trainers. And a guinea pig. And a tool kit. And an iPod. And some of David Walliams's books."

"—herds pie," Ruby would say.

"For dinner, I said, Sam," his dad would say. "Not for your birthday."

Obviously, Sam wouldn't always say *these* things (and so, obviously, the people he was speaking to wouldn't always say *those* things back). No. Sometimes it would be a different type of cake, a different style of party and a different list of presents (although always including a telescope: Sam was a big fan of *Star Trek*, and sci-fi generally, and wanted to see as much of the solar system as he could from the window of his room in order to watch out for visiting aliens). Which did mean that he had ended up with a very long present list, and a very long selection of party-theme ideas. Which, in turn, presented a bit of a problem for his mum and dad, both in terms of choice and in terms of money, because they didn't have a lot of that.

But the thing that never changed was Sam's excitement about the day.

And then, finally, it came.

CHAPTER 2
UM . . .

"**O**h, Mum! Dad! That was amazing! What an amazing day!" Sam was saying as he undressed in his bedroom. It was 10pm on Saturday the eighth of September. The last of his friends, all of whom went to Bracket Wood, the local primary school, had left. Vicky and Charlie were smiling at him.

"So! Did you like your party?" said Vicky.

"Yes! Especially the sci-fi cake! In the shape of

the *Starship Enterprise*! With six different gobstoppers for planets all round it! And candy Klingons and other aliens on the sides! Great idea, Mum!"

"Yes, well, it was *your* idea, Sam . . . I think it was cake suggestion number four – you made it last Monday . . ."

"And the film-theme fancy dress really worked, didn't it, Dad? Everyone's costume was great! Barry Bennett looked brilliant as Gru from *Despicable Me*! And Ellie and Fred Stone as Minions! And Malcolm Bailey as the sloth from *Zootropolis*! And Morris Fawcett as Homer Simpson!"

"Well," said Charlie, "that was your idea too. Party suggestion number seven "

"And you looked great!" said Vicky, grimacing as she pulled off Sam's Wall-E head and feet.

"Well, that's why I won the Best Costume Prize . . ."

"No, actually, that's because it was *your* party," said Ruby, wandering into the room. She'd been allowed to stay up a little bit later as it was Sam's birthday. Ruby had a tendency to be very direct about everything, in a seven-year-old way. But she *was* a very clever seven-year-old. "So everyone thought you had to win. In fact, Mum and Dad basically bribed all your friends to vote for you by giving them extra cake and—"

"Yes, all right, Ruby. Time to clean your teeth," said Charlie, taking her hand, and leading her – a little forcefully – towards the door.

"Dad? Mum? For my birthday, can I have a kitten?" said Ruby as she was leaving the room, books tucked under her arm, to do extra homework as usual. This was another thing Ruby said a lot, as well as "actually". Sometimes she combined them and said, "Actually, Mum and Dad, can I have a kitten?" Even when no one had asked her what she wanted.

"Well . . ." said Vicky.

"Um . . ." said Charlie.

Ruby didn't look surprised. She was used to her mum and dad saying "um . . ." in answer to the kitten question. But that didn't mean she was going to let it go, either.

"Sam got a guinea pig," she said, pointedly. "Spock!" Which, indeed, was something else on

Sam's birthday list that his parents had managed to get him. They looked over to said guinea pig, in its cage on the floor. It was a brown-and-white one, with a little tuft on its head. Sam had decided to call the guinea pig Spock after the extremely logical, cold character in *Star Trek*. Spock looked back at them with quite a strong sense of, "I think that name is very unfair."

"Ruby," said Charlie, "you know what a kitten will become?"

"Yes, actually, I do, Dad. I'm seven, not an idiot. A *cat*."

"OK, so a grown cat, unlike Spock, will need some outside space. We haven't got any."

"Yes, we have," said Ruby, pointing to the window. "What's all that stuff out there?"

"Oh right. I see. Is the cat going to go down by itself from the seventeenth floor? In the lift that smells of wee?"

Ruby sighed, as if that question was ridiculous. Which it kind of was.

"We'll think about it," said Mum.

"Um . . ." said Dad.

Ruby nodded, feeling her point had been made, and turned to go out of the room. "Night, Sam! Hope you had a great birthday!"

"I did!" he replied.

CHAPTER 3
THE STAR-WATCHER EXPLORER

Sam looked up at his mum. She was buttoning his new pyjamas, which were covered in little UFOs. Sam, of course, being eleven, could do up his own pyjama buttons. But he knew it was something his mum still liked to do. "And I loved all my presents! The skateboard and the computer games and the new trainers and the DIY tool kit and the books . . ."

"Everything on your list," said Vicky. "Well, apart from

the iPod. Sorry about that, Sam. Maybe next year . . ."

"It doesn't matter, Mum. You got me the telescope. That was my big present. I love it!"

They looked over to the window. There it was: the Star-Watcher Explorer. Sam's dad had already set it up on a tripod, and angled it against the window, pointing at the moon. It was black and sleek and long, with a computerised tracker to allow Sam to find particular constellations.

Sam and his family lived in a tower block – Noam Chomsky House – on the seventeenth floor. So it was the best present ever! They were so high up that Sam had an uninterrupted view of the night sky, and all its stars.

"You should be able to see any aliens out there with that, eh, Sam?" said Charlie.

"I don't think so!" shouted a voice from outside the room. It was Ruby's. "Actually, the nearest planet capable of sustaining life is four light years away!"

"How far is that?" said Sam. "In miles?"

There was a silence. But only for a few seconds.
"Two hundred and thirty-five billion billion. Give or
take the odd mile."

"Um . . . OK . . ." said Charlie. "But we don't know
how fast their spacecrafts travel, do we?"

"Well, anyway," said Vicky, looking out of the
window at the night sky above the city, "I just
have a feeling that there *is* life out there somewhere."

Charlie smiled: he knew that his wife had a lot of
faith in her feelings. He loved that about her, even if
he didn't have so much faith in her feelings.

"Is that like the feeling," he said, putting his arm
round her, "you had yesterday, about how I shouldn't
walk under that ladder – and so I didn't, and fell in
that huge puddle instead?"

She pushed him away, but smiled as she did it.

"It didn't cost too much, did it?" asked Sam,

going over to the telescope.

Sam's dad was a manager at HomeFront, a big building supplies store, and his mum worked at home, buying and selling stuff on the internet, so they weren't exactly rich – though it did also mean that Dad had been able to get a staff discount on the tool kit, something Sam had really wanted, as he loved making and fixing things.

"Don't worry about that!" said Vicky. "It's your birthday!" She looked over at the telescope. "Are the stars out? If you see a shooting one, you can wish on it! You *should* wish on it!"

"Really?" said Sam. "Does that actually, y'know . . . work?"

"Yes!" said Vicky confidently.

Charlie looked at her, and raised an eyebrow.

"Well. No one really knows. Do they?" she said defiantly.

"Um . . ." said Charlie, bending down and checking

the telescope lens. "Well. What I *would* say is that tonight is too cloudy to see the stars anyway."

"Never mind," said Sam. "We'll look through it tomorrow!"

He climbed up the little ladder and got into bed. It was a bunk bed, and sometimes Sam would show how good he was at balancing on that ladder by walking up without using his hands, although tonight he was too tired for that.

"Oh! And I liked it when the grans and grandpas came round for lunch," he said. "They didn't even fight!"

"I know," said Vicky, clearly surprised herself. "They were on their best behaviour."

"Yes . . ." said Sam, settling his head on the pillow. "Grandpa Sam didn't even swear at Grandpa Mike. And Grandpa Mike didn't even punch him or threaten to get his boys on him or anything. And Grandma Glenda and Grandma Poppy even smiled at each other."

"I think that might have been a snarl . . ." said his dad.

"Shush, Charlie. Anyway . . . you should go to sleep now, Sammy," said Sam's mum. "I imagine you're exhausted . . ."

"Specially," said his dad, "having got up at the dot of six in the morning!"

"Was that the time?" said Sam.

"Well. It was one minute past six when you were knocking on our bedroom door, demanding presents. I'm sure of that . . ."

"But that was my favourite bit!" said Sam.

"Of what?"

"Of my birthday! I love how exciting it is to wake up on your birthday! And realise that it *is* your birthday! This day you've been waiting for, for so long, it's finally here!"

"Yes," said Vicky. "That is very exciting."

"Not quite as exciting when you get to forty-three,

though," said Charlie, and Vicky laughed at his joke in a grown-ups-laughing-at-grown-ups'-stuff kind of way.

"Isn't it?" said Sam.

"Pardon?" said Charlie.

"Exciting. Isn't it exciting any more, your birthday?"

His mum and dad looked at each other.

"Well," said Vicky, looking back at Sam kindly, and pulling his duvet back across him. "It's always nice, yes. But maybe not quite as nice as it was when you're ten . . . or when that of course turns into eleven."

Sam nodded, but then shook his head.

"I'd like it to be my birthday every day!" he said.

His parents smiled, and then both of them got on the bed with him – climbed up the ladder and everything – and put their arms round him, something that in this family was referred to as a bundle-hug.

"Wait for me!" said Ruby as she hurried back into the room. She climbed up and joined the bundle-hug. She was holding a big science textbook, which made it a bit uncomfortable.

Then, after that, Vicky said:

"I'm glad the day went so well. Ruby, back to your room. Sam, time to go to sleep . . ."

And Sam smiled at her, and shut his eyes.

CHAPTER 4
11.59PM

Normally, Sam had no problem sleeping. Normally, he was out as soon as his head hit the pillow. And his parents were right: he should have been more ready for sleep than ever, given how early he'd been up that morning.

But his birthday had been so great, and he was still so excited, that Sam just couldn't sleep. He found himself tossing and turning in his bed, thinking of how much he just wanted to stay up and play with all his presents.

Also, he thought, looking at the numbers on the clock by his bedside – 10.24 – *it's still my birthday! For another hour and thirty-six minutes! What am I thinking of, going to sleep?*

No – he also thought – *I should be up, doing birthday stuff!*

So Sam got out of bed. And tried on his trainers. And ran on the spot with them for a little while. Then he stood on his skateboard, which was great: his parents had splashed out on it – it was exactly the one he wanted, a flexiboard, customised with cool silver wheels and the right trucks and everything.

It would have been more fun to ride on it outside, obviously, but even in his quite small bedroom Sam was able to do some 360s and some frontside flips. Then he got Spock the guinea pig out of his cage, and did some more 360s, but this time with the guinea pig balanced on his head. The guinea pig didn't look that keen on this. In fact, he looked down at his new master with quite a strong sense of, "If it's all going to be like this, I'm going to be escaping to Peru. Which is where guinea pigs come from. In case you don't know. Which I get the impression you don't."

(He had a pretty expressive face for a guinea pig, Spock. Which made him somewhat different, it has to be said, from the original Spock.)

Then, he – Sam, not Spock – ate some of the leftover marshmallow from the cake that his mum had brought up on a plate. Then he read the first few chapters of *Demon Dentist*, which was very funny.

After thirty pages, Sam looked over at the clock, which said, now, 11.55pm. He still, amazingly, didn't feel that tired. What he did feel was a bit sad. Mainly, he felt a bit sad that his birthday was ending, officially, now. He sat up, and said to Spock, who was lying on his chest – had, in fact, tumbled down into his lap as a result of him sitting up – "Oh, Spock! I wish it was my birthday every day."

Spock looked up at him with quite a strong sense of, "I wish I could live in a cage made out of parsley, but we can't have everything."

Just at that point, though, a light fell across the room. Sam looked up to see that the source of the light was beyond his bedroom curtains. Moonlight.

Aha! he thought. *If I can see moonlight, the clouds must have parted. And, if the clouds have parted, I can use my telescope!*

So Sam got out of bed and moved over to the window. He drew the curtains, and looked out.

He was right. It was no longer a cloudy night. Noam Chomsky House stood on a hill, and the road from it ran down, after a few miles, to the river that wound through the city. Sometimes, when – like now – the sky was clear and the moon came out, Sam could see all the way to the river (even without a telescope); he could even see the reflection of the moonlight on the water, lighting up a small tree-filled island that sat between the banks.

But Sam wasn't interested in looking down at the water. He wanted to look up at the sky. He wanted to look up at the sky through his telescope, and see the stars and the moon. All of which were suddenly out.

He put his eye to the lenspiece at the bottom end of the telescope. It was hard to see anything – all he could make out, in fact, was what appeared to be three or four massive spider legs, which at first, excitedly, he thought must be aliens but then realised were just his eyelashes. Gradually, though, his vision got used to it, and then he could see the moon!

All white and shining and pockmarked, like Grandpa Sam's face (although that was only the pockmarked bit, as Grandpa Sam's face was sort of leathery and brown, and, though friendly, very rarely shining).

"I can see the moon, Spock!" he said to Spock, who was now on the floor, by his cage. Spock looked back at him with quite a strong sense of, "When you can see a planet made of parsley, let me know. Meanwhile, open my house, please."

When Sam turned back to the telescope, though, he couldn't see the moon through it any more. This was a thing about telescopes: even small eye movements meant that you could end up a long way from what you'd been looking at before. He scanned right, left, up and down, but couldn't see where the moon had gone – and then—

What was *that*? A spaceship? It was black, and oblong, and had a series of enormous flickering green numbers on the front of it . . .

. . . Oh. It was his clock. Made to look much bigger and more spaceship-ey because he was seeing it through the telescope. He'd turned the thing all the way round, away from the window, and was looking back towards his bed.

Feeling a little silly, Sam began to move the telescope back round again. But not before noticing that the time was about to turn – the 59 of 11:59 had been there for a while – to midnight. And then his birthday really would be properly over. He sighed, shook his head and looked through the lenspiece for one last sight of the stars.

And then he saw it.

CHAPTER 5

WHEN YOU WISH UPON A STAR

A shooting star! A really big one, tearing up the sky! Through the telescope, it looked amazing, like a comet, or a rocket, or a firework. And it didn't just go in a split second, like shooting stars do: no. It stayed travelling across the night sky for what seemed like ages, in a long arc from one end of the horizon to the other.

It was astonishing, beautiful. Sam couldn't believe he was the only person in the world seeing it: surely NASA, or Jodrell Bank, or Brian Cox, or someone from the Star Wars Resistance, was also watching. But he didn't think about that for too long, because – while the star was still shooting across his vision – he remembered what his mum had said.

You can *wish* upon a star. You *should* wish upon a star.

Sam wasn't superstitious. In fact, he had been pretty tongue-in-cheek about it when saying to his mum, just as she was putting him to bed, "Does that actually work?" But this was different. This was a star so bright, and so fast, and so present in the sky that it really did feel to him that it might be magical.

And so – he wasn't to know this, because he was looking through the telescope – on the stroke of midnight (it wasn't actually a stroke: it was a small, almost silent click, as 11:59 became 12:00 on his clock) – he said, out loud, towards the star:

"I wish it could be my birthday every day!"

At which point the star seemed to burst into even greater light – it seemed to *glow*, extra-brightly, for a second – and then it fell from the sky, straight down. Sam tried to follow it with his telescope, and for a moment he could, even though it was travelling really quickly. This star looked as if it was on a mission to come to Earth! Or as if someone had shot it out of the sky! Perhaps, unbeknownst to Sam, his telescope was mounted with a laser beam that had blasted into the heart of it!

Unfortunately, these thoughts got in the way, and meant that Sam couldn't track the journey of the star all the way down. It appeared – but this couldn't be right – to land in the middle of the river, either in the water itself, or maybe on one of the islands. Sam could see one of these through the telescope. But it was dark, and covered in trees, and definitely not lit up by a falling celestial object.

Sam lifted his eye from the lenspiece. He looked around. Nothing, it had to be said, very magical appeared to have happened. His room, with its posters of the *Starship Enterprise* and *Battlestar Galactica*, was the same. On the floor stood his new skateboard, and trainers, and book, and guinea pig. Who was looking at him with quite a strong sense of, "Wishing on a star? Who are you – Jiminy Cricket?"

Sam felt a tiny bit disappointed. Not being superstitious, there was no real reason for him to think that wishing on a star would have any effect, but he had somehow felt wishing on *this* star, being so bright, would mean something. *Clearly*, he thought, *I was wrong there*.

Never mind, he thought, and went over, picked Spock up, gave him a quick stroke, opened the cage and put him inside.

"Happy birthday, Sam," he said to himself, one last time.

Then he realised he was, at last, tired, and so went up his little ladder to his top bunk bed, shut his eyes and fell asleep, immediately.

CHAPTER 6
BIRTHDAY TWO

KNOCK-KNOCK!

It must be Ruby, Sam assumed. She still got up really early, like little kids do. So he just ignored it.

But then the knock came again. And, to be honest, it sounded a bit too . . . full, and high on the door, to be Ruby. It sounded like an adult's knock.

He stretched his arms, and sat up.

"Sam! Sam-my . . . !" came his mum's voice, from behind the door.

"Hey, Sam!" came his dad's voice, as well.

It *was* his mum. *And* his dad. So why were they up, and waking *him* up, so early on a Sunday morning?

Well, there was an easy enough way to find out. Sam got out of bed, climbed down the ladder and opened the door . . . to see his mum, dad and sister standing there with a tray, on which lay a full English breakfast, a glass of lemonade and a doughnut. Around the plate were eleven candles. Sam looked up, frowning. They were all smiling.

"Happy birthday!" they all said as one.

"Sorry?" said Sam.

"Happy birthday! We've made you breakfast in bed!" said Vicky.

"Your favourite! Full English! With lemonade and a doughnut!" said Charlie.

"Yes!" said Ruby. "Not very healthy! Actually."

Sam watched, amazed, as they marched in. His mum reached up to the top bunk and placed the tray on his bed. Then she went over to the window and opened the curtains.

"Come on, Sam! Back to bed, and tuck in!" she said.

Sam shook his head, but smiled.

"Well . . . OK . . . thanks. Is this a joke?"

"What?" said Vicky. "No, I've made it exactly as you like it . . ."

"No, I can see that," he said. "It looks lovely . . . but it's *not* my birthday! That was yesterday."

"Well," said Charlie. "That was the anniversary of the day you were actually born, yes."

"But we woke up this morning," said Vicky, "both with exactly the same words in our head. And those words were: 'Happy birthday, Sam!' And it made me think: there's no reason to celebrate your birth just on that date because *every day* we're happy that you were born! So we should celebrate it every day!"

"She's right," said Charlie. "I woke up with those exact words going round and round in my head too. 'Happy birthday, Sam!' And I figured, why not?"

"*Really?*" said Sam.

Vicky nodded. "I know you were thinking the same thing, Charlie. In fact, I had a *feeling*."

"Um . . ." said Charlie. But he was nodding, and looking a little surprised at himself for going along so fully with one of Vicky's feelings.

"It happened to me too, actually," said Ruby. "I woke up, and the first thing I thought was, 'Happy birthday, Sam!'"

"So we went straight downstairs and started making you your birthday breakfast in bed!" said Vicky.

Sam nodded. He looked out of the window. He walked over, in fact, to the window. The view was the same as ever: the estate, and then the roads and houses leading down to the river. There was no sign that anything amazing or magical or . . . *starry* had happened during the night.

"We should celebrate my birthday . . ." he said, still looking out of the window, "every day?"

"Every day," said his mum.

"Every day," said his dad.

"Every day. Actually," said – most surprisingly – his sister.

Which made Sam think about something. He'd spotted a flaw in what they were saying.

"What about . . . Ruby?" he said. "Why aren't we celebrating *her* birthday . . . every day?"

Charlie and Vicky frowned. They looked at Ruby. Ruby looked back at them. Then Vicky's face cleared.

"Well, we *will* do. When she's eleven. That'll be when we have the same thought about her. It'll be a family tradition, I imagine."

"Yes! That's right! You're all right with that, aren't you, Rube?" said Sam.

"Fine," said Ruby. "It's only four years. Which, as I'm sure you know, to a child of seven, seems only like about four hundred."

"Er . . . right," said Mum.

But then Charlie said: "Great! OK, I'm off out!"

"Where to?" said Sam.

"Never you mind . . ." his dad replied, with a nod and a wink at Vicky, who smiled back. Which, Sam knew, was grown-up code – really obvious grown-up code – for, "I'm going to go and buy Sam some presents."

His dad left the room, and Sam looked back at his smiling mum and somewhat less smiling sister. Could it be real? Could the wish he made last night have come true?

"Come on, Sam," said his mum. "It's not going to be here forever . . ."

Sam frowned at her. "My birthday?"

"No! That *is* going to be here forever. I meant: your breakfast!"

And it did smell, it had to be said, very tempting, especially the mix of bacon and doughnut. So Sam said: "Thanks, Mum!" and scampered up the bunk-bed ladder, and tucked in.

CHAPTER 7
EVERYDAY MAGICAL

"You what? You what? You what?" said Grandpa Sam, later that day.

"Ah, now, you see, you – stupid – 'ave started to say things over and over again," said Grandpa Mike. "You old fool! You 'ave gone completely gaga."

"Me, gaga? You're the one that's gaga! You, in fact, *are* Lady Gaga!" said Grandpa Sam.

"Oh. What a good joke. You should be doin' a blinkin' comedy act with material like that. Hang on,

I'll phone Michael McIntyre and tell him 'e may as well retire."

"Oh, shut up," said Grandpa Sam. "You boom-donking dipthong!"

Grandpa Sam swore a lot. But luckily it was all swearwords he made up, so it's OK for you to hear them. *Fudgeblaster*, *piggle-dandler*, *dungpie*, *snotbum* (OK that one is getting quite close to real swearing), *blobnoodler* and *great big fragglestooping bustyplop* were all in his repertoire.

Secretly – if you ever meet the others, don't tell them – Grandpa Sam was Sam's favourite grandparent. It was partly because Sam was named after him, and partly because Grandpa Sam was the first person apart from his parents who saw him on the day he was born, but mainly because of the funny swearwords. Whenever he did one – like now, when saying *boomdonking dipthong* – he would wink at Sam (and Ruby), as if to let them know they were in on the joke.

"*You* shut up!" said Grandpa Mike. "I'll do yer if you call me stuff like that! I will! I'll do yer!"

Grandpa Mike didn't swear as much as Grandpa Sam, but he did speak in an accent that sounded as if it came from an old British film, and he waved his fists around a lot and suggested he was going to fight people (mainly Grandpa Sam). This was because he thought of himself, even though he was seventy-seven, as hard.

As a tough guy. He sometimes referred, with a dark air of mystery, to time spent in his earlier life "inside". Which sometimes means prison, which is what Grandpa Mike *wanted* you to think. But what he actually meant *was* inside. His house. Because he didn't much like going out.

Grandpa Sam reacted to Grandpa Mike's aggression by whistling a happy tune. Which he always did when Grandpa Mike got cross, which only made Grandpa Mike more furious.

"Shut your whistle 'ole! I said I'll do yer."

"He will! That's right! Don't call my husband stupid names!" said Grandma Glenda to Grandpa Sam. She was married – as you may have been able to work out – to Grandpa Mike.

"Don't you tell *my* husband not to tell *your* husband to shut up!" said Grandma Poppy, who – I don't have to tell you this, do I? – was married to Grandpa Sam. Poppy was very thin. She ate an awful lot of sponge cake, and toffees, and biscuits with jam in the middle, and other stuff that old people like, but without ever putting on weight.

This was not true of Grandma Glenda, who ate virtually nothing – constantly counting calories, and demanding no butter on her bread, and refusing pudding unless it was the dullest puddings, rice ones with skimmed milk and NO JAM, for example – but was shaped not unlike a large balloon. Although one filled with flesh, rather than air.

"Oh yeah?" said Grandma Glenda, getting up from her chair and leaning over the table and putting her face very close to Grandma Poppy's. "And who's going to stop me?"

"I am!" said Vicky, coming into the living room with a teapot. "Come on, Mum, Dad, Glenda, Mike . . . We're not going to be fighting today, remember, because" – and here she glanced significantly in Sam's direction – "it's a *special* day."

All the grandparents looked at each other.

"Oh yes!" they said at once. "Happy birthday, Sam!" they chorused.

"Yes, it's strange," said Grandma Poppy. "We all woke up with those words in our heads, didn't we?"

"I suppose so," said Grandma Glenda, as if it was hard to agree with Grandma Poppy about anything. "Well, I mean, yes, we did. All of us."

Then they folded their arms and sat back in their chairs and did their best to smile at each other.

That was when Sam really started to believe it was true. Because what his grandparents *usually* liked to do, when they came round, was fight. And shout and swear at each other.

The only days they *didn't* do that were his birthday, and Ruby's birthday. He knew it wasn't Ruby's birthday. So it must be his birthday. Again. Today.

For a second, it bothered him that his mum had referred to today as a special day. Because if it was a special day, what did that make the day before, which had been Sam's *real* birthday?

But, then again, today was feeling *pretty* real, birthday-wise. His dad had come back from the shops with loads of new presents. Stuff left over from his birthday list that he hadn't got the day before. A chess set, a lava lamp, two video games, three new T-shirts and a pair of headphones! Wireless, with Bluetooth, and noise reduction! Plus his mum had nipped out when his dad had got back and got him a book to go with his telescope, with maps of stars and constellations to find and check against the night sky.

And his grandparents had brought him presents too! Rubbish ones, of course, but they always did that. Well, not rubbish ones – ones that they would have got when they were children, basically. Grandma Poppy had got him a pipe that blew bubbles; Grandpa Sam gave him an old watch, which he said he'd like to see him – Sam – wear every day; and Grandpa Mike and Grandma Glenda had got him a pack of cards with which you could play Happy Families. So . . . yes, rubbish ones.

But Sam still thought: *Well, it's not actually going to be like a birthday. Yes, I've got presents, and, yes, my mum brought me breakfast in bed, and, yes, my grandparents aren't fighting, but it's not—* and then the doorbell rang.

"Who's that?" said Sam.

"Why don't you go and see?" said his dad.

Sam shrugged, and went to the door, assuming that it would be the man with the shaven head and the tattoos on his face who sold dusters and kitchen cloths for £10 each and had a card saying he'd recently come out of prison. He often came round on a Sunday afternoon.

But, as Sam approached the door, he could tell that it wasn't him. It looked like a much bigger person, with about ten strange heads. When he opened the door, though, it wasn't a much bigger

person with about ten heads. It was Finn and Jake and the Ice Queen and . . . and a whole bunch of other characters from *Adventure Time!* And, weirdly, Richard the rabbit dad from *The Amazing World of Gumball*.

"Oh!" said Sam, with some surprise.

"Happy birthday again, Sam!" chorused Finn and Jake and the Ice Queen from *Adventure Time*. And Richard the dad from *The Amazing World of Gumball*.

Except it wasn't actually them. This story isn't that magical (it's more . . . *everyday* magical). It was all Sam's friends from Bracket Wood, in costume: Barry and Lukas and Taj and Fred and Ellie and Morris and Isla. It was Morris who'd got it wrong and dressed as Richard.

"Oh!" said Sam again. "Come—"

He was going to say "in". But by then everyone had already piled in, rushing past his astonished face.

CHAPTER 8
NEW KID

After the party was over, Sam realised he hadn't properly had time, what with all the second-birthday-in-two-days activity, to play with his skateboard. So, while it was still light, he took the lift down to ground level, holding his board.

The lift at Noam Chomsky House was a massive silver (not *real* silver, obviously: painted silver) box. It smelt not unlike a big toilet, particularly in one corner, and when they all took the lift together Sam and Ruby would always try to push each other into that bit. And it creaked a lot. But Sam didn't mind that. It got him to the bottom all right, and on the ground outside the tower block there were loads of concreted-over areas, some of which had humps and tunnels and ramps that made it almost like a little skate park.

The lift doors opened, and Sam got on to his board and skated out to the concrete. He sailed easily over the paved path, and then down one of the ramps into a small bowl-like section, which cut underneath the main tower. It was a touch grim in there – sometimes Sam felt that it looked like a place where one of those crime dramas that his parents watched on TV would have their final big shootout scene – but it was the best part for skateboarding. Then he stopped. Because someone was already there.

It was a kid about his own age, but a little smaller.

He had cropped short hair, and dark skin, and wore a grey hoody. But these things were not important. What was important was that he was an *amazing* skater. Alpha flips, Ollie norths, Ollie souths, 720s, spins, tail grabs, pull-ups – he could do them all. He made the grim bowl-like area under Noam Chomsky House feel like a skate park in one of those places Sam had seen on YouTube, in America or wherever, where the sky always seemed to be blue and the wheels and helmets of the skaters dazzled in the sun.

Sam watched for a while, awestruck. Then the boy must've noticed him, because he flipped the board round, and skated effortlessly towards him. At which point, Sam noticed that, despite being a brilliant skater, this kid was not riding a brilliant board. It was scratched and battered, and although that did make it look kind of cool, the wheels were pitted, the grip-tape was worn out, the trucks were bent and none of the parts were from any top-level brands.

And then, looking up from the board, Sam noticed something else. The skater wasn't a boy. He was a girl.

"Hello!" she said.

"Hi," said Sam. "Do you live round here?"

"Yes," said the girl. She had a strong accent, which Sam couldn't place, but sounded similar to the way frightened people spoke on the news in reports from countries that always seemed to be at war. Except she didn't sound frightened. "Fifteenth floor. My family were just placed here. By the government. I don't know how long we will be staying."

"Oh right," said Sam. "You're a great skater."

"Thanks," she said. "Where I come from, we had to stop going to school. And we lived near a car park, but no cars ever came there any more. So just to keep me busy my father" – and here she held the board up, a little apologetically, as if knowing it wasn't quite as flash as it should be – "he built me this board and I went to the car park every day and learnt a lot of tricks."

"Why?"

"Why what?"

"Why did you stop going to school?"

"Because the school was bombed."

"Oh . . ." said Sam, feeling a bit stupid, because up to that point he'd quite liked the sound of not having to go to school.

"That's OK," the girl said. "Hey! Who wants to go to school?"

Which made Sam laugh. But she was too busy looking down at his new present to notice. "Nice board . . ."

"Thanks. Do you want to have a go?" he said, holding out his shiny and sparkling new board. "Sorry . . . I don't know your name . . . ?"

"My name is Zada. And *you* should try out your board first. It's your birthday, isn't it?"

Sam stared at her. "How do you know that?"

Zada frowned. "I'm not sure. Good guess, I suppose."

Sam considered saying, "Well, now that my birthday might be happening every day, you were on fairly safe ground with that guess," but thought that might be a bit complicated for a girl he'd just met.

"OK," he said instead, and kicked off. He felt a little nervous, actually, skating in front of someone who was so good. He tried a few of his more limited tricks, but as he went round the bowl, he went too fast, and ended up falling off.

Zada was really nice about it, though.

"Doesn't matter," she said. "Get back on! Keep going! Just move your weight more gently . . . yes! That is right . . . !"

She kept shouting encouragement, helping Sam

through the turn of the bowl, and down again. And, as night started to fall, and the streetlights started to come on around the estate, Sam relaxed into his skateboarding stride, and learnt from this new expert he'd just met.

It was one of the best parts of this, his second birthday of the year.

CHAPTER 9
THIS COULD GET COMPLICATED

As Sam tucked into his third birthday breakfast in three mornings, and saw his mum and dad smiling at him (although the smiles were rather tired – it had been a long party the day before, and his parents must have been up late wrapping all his new presents, because there was a whole new batch sitting in front of Sam on the bedclothes, all tied up with coloured ribbon), he wondered how far, basically, he could push this.

"So . . ." he said, washing down a delicious bit of doughnut and bacon with a gulp of lemonade, "I don't think I fancy going to school today."

"Oh!" said Sam's mum. "Really?"

"Yes," he said. "After all, it *is* my birthday."

His parents glanced at each other.

"Um . . ." said Charlie. "Of course it is."

"Every day is your birthday," said Vicky. Sam looked up at her as she said this, to see if there was a hint of any undertone in her expression – sarcasm, or jokiness, or just uncertainty – but there wasn't.

"You do normally go to school on your birthday . . ." Charlie continued, "if it's a school day."

"I know . . ." said Sam, "but – thanks, Mum! Thanks, Dad!" He'd unwrapped the first of today's presents – a big electric toy car with remote control – ". . . I don't think it's fair."

"What?" said Vicky.

"To have to go to school on my birthday."

"Actually, I went to school on my birthday this year," said Ruby, coming into the room. "My *one* birthday."

Sam nodded. He'd noticed that whatever magic was making everyone – including Ruby – accept that his birthday was happening every day, it hadn't stopped his sister from being quite annoyed about it.

"OK," said Sam. "But did that feel fair?"

". . . No," said Ruby, after the tiniest second of thought.

"And also," said Sam, "if I'm going to be having my birthday every day, I should be able to mix it up a bit. Otherwise most days are going to be the same."

His parents looked at each other.

Vicky shrugged. "Well, I suppose I could call the school and ask if they'll let you have the day off."

"Is that . . . legal?" said Charlie.

"Not without permission from the head teacher, actually," said Ruby. She was, as I say, quite advanced for a seven-year-old.

"OK. But I think Mr Fawcett" – that was the head teacher – "won't mind if I tell him it's just for this one . . . special . . . day."

At that point Sam's parents looked at each other again. They were both thinking the same thing: *Oh. It's not just this one special day. It's every day. This could get complicated.* "Great!" said Sam. "And then you'd better call *work*, and ask them if *they'll* let you have the day off . . ."

"This could get complicated," said Sam's dad.

But this birthday, at least, wasn't that complicated.

First a theme park, then Five Guys for lunch, then go-karting in the afternoon, then the new Pixar movie, then Byron for dinner (Sam liked burgers). It was a great day. There was a slightly difficult moment when Vicky and Charlie had a row about paying the bill at Byron, where they'd had to have a cake, as well, of course, but by the time they got home it was all forgotten.

CHAPTER 10
THE WHOLE SCHOOL

The next day, Sam went to school. He hadn't been sure about this — he'd thought about demanding another day off, seeing as it was, after all, his birthday — but then remembered that every day was now his birthday, and decided he couldn't stay off school every day.

When he got to school, though, things weren't quite as they usually were. As he arrived, he could see there was an enormous banner placed on top of the main gate. Getting closer, he saw that it said:

HAPPY BIRTHDAY, SAM!!

And just to make sure no one confused him with any of the other Sams at Bracket Wood Primary School it said underneath·

(Green, 6B)

Then, when Sam walked into the playground, the whole school was there! The school orchestra – actually just five children, with a violin, a guitar, two recorders and a pair of cymbals – started playing the opening chords to "Happy Birthday"! Everyone joined in: even Reception, who, like all Reception kids, didn't really know the words or the tune, and, obviously, one of them was crying.

At the end of it, Mr Fawcett, the head teacher, came forward with an enormous cake. It also had the words "Happy birthday, Sam (Green, 6B)" on the top, and a figure with his arms in the air that looked like a man who, some time ago, had melted.

"Here you are, Sam!" he said.

"Thank you, Mr Fawcett . . ." said Sam, bemused. "Is that a clay model of . . . me?"

"Yes. It was made by that boy in Reception. The one who's crying." Mr Fawcett looked at the boy, and then at the clay model. "Sorry," he said.

"It's fine," said Sam. "Thank you." It did occur to Sam to ask Mr Fawcett why they hadn't made anything like this fuss *last* year on the eighth of September, when he'd had to go to school on his actual birthday. But the idea of that day being his *actual* birthday was fading in his mind, so he forgot about it, and blew the candles out.

The whole school went, "Hooray!"

"Make a wish?" said Mr Fawcett.

"Um . . . no, that seems a bit pointless," said Sam. "Seeing as my birthday's happening every day now . . ."

"Oh! Yes! We don't want to be greedy, do we? Wish-wise!" said Mr Fawcett.

Sam nodded. Then another thought occurred to him.

"Um . . . did you have all this ready to do yesterday . . . ? When I didn't come?"

Mr Fawcett looked slightly embarrassed. As did Mr Barrington, the deputy head, and Sam's form teacher. As did the orchestra. And everyone else there.

"Yes!" shouted the crying boy. Tearfully.

"It was the oddest thing," said Mr Fawcett. "I woke up yesterday morning with some words in my head, and those words were, 'Happy birthday, Sam!' And I thought, *Why not make it his birthday every day?*"

"So did I!" said Barry Bennett.

"And me!" said Malcolm Bailey.

"Us too," said Fred and Ellie Stone.

"So we all got everything ready," continued Mr Fawcett. "And again today."

"Oh, sorry, everybody!" said Sam.

"No problem, really. After all, we're going to be doing some sort of celebration for you every day from now on . . ."

"Shall I cut the cake?" asked Sam, looking around for a knife.

"Well, no," said Mr Fawcett. "You are not – in fact, no pupils are – allowed to eat any of it. Not on school grounds. Due to new dietary rules established by Jamie Oliver."

Sam thought for a moment. Then he said: "But . . . it's my birthday!"

Mr Fawcett frowned. He glanced over at Mr Barrington, who shrugged.

"Oh, all right, then!" he said. And the whole school tucked in. With their hands. Which meant the crying boy stopped crying.

CHAPTER 11
HODGEPODGE

When Sam got to his class, Mr Barrington, who was also his form teacher, said:

"Right! OK!"

He used his usual schoolmasterly tone, but then found himself saying – almost against his will, it seemed: it was like someone else was *making* him say it – something *not* very schoolmasterly.

"So. Right. Well . . . because it's Sam's birthday again today" – he glanced at Sam, who was sitting at the front of the class – "he is going to choose what subjects we do!"

"Really?" said Sam.

"Yes," said Mr Barrington, although he looked as surprised as everyone else about it. "Ahem. I suppose. I seem to have said so now, anyway. So. What would you like? English? Maths? History? DT?"

Sam thought about it for a moment. He was beginning to realise something about the way this worked. Something powerful.

"Silly Words!" he said.

"I beg your pardon?"

"Silly Words!" said Sam. "A lesson on which words and phrases are the silliest!"

A noise came up from the rest of the class. One that sounded like a combination of "Yes!", "Definitely!", "That sounds fun!" and "Let's do that!"

Sam wasn't sure where that idea had come from, although if he had to pin it down it was probably something to do with Grandpa Sam and his funny swearing.

"No, no. I meant . . . you know . . . the usual subjects . . ." said Mr Barrington.

Sam raised his eyebrows and said what he was now starting to realise were the magic words.

"But, sir: it's my *birthday*."

"Bottom!" said Morris. For the fifth time.

"I've told you, Morris, we're not allowing rude words."

"Bottom isn't a rude word, Mr Barrington!" said Fred.

"Well, it *can* be . . ."

Mr Barrington held his magic marker up to the whiteboard. The way the lesson worked was this: members of 6B put their hands up, said a silly word and, if the general response was that the word was silly enough, Mr Barrington wrote it down on the board. In no particular order, although there was a sense that at the end of the lesson there would be a vote on the silliest. Word, that is.

So far, written up, were the words:

stickleback
portion
muckle
knickers (just got under the rude bar, apparently)
ballyhoo
stinky
nosehole
flappy
blubber
hodgepodge
shrub

"Lukas?" said Mr Barrington, in response to a hand going up.

"Fart?"

"Definitely rude," said Mr Barrington. "Ellie?"

"Puddleduck?"

"Hmm. That's a name."

"Of a duck, sir."

"Yes. But still. A name. A surname, in fact. Are we allowed proper nouns, Sam?"

"Sir," said Sam, "it's your lesson. I just suggested the topic . . ."

Mr Barrington considered for a moment. A part of him seemed pleased that, at least, in amongst all the silly wordage, there had been a moment of grammar.

"I think . . . not," he said. "Any more for any more?"

"BOTTOM!"

"That's it, Morris! Detention!"

CHAPTER 12

A PACKET OF WERTHER'S ORIGINALS, SOME SHOELACES AND A JAR OF DURAGLIT

A few days later, Sam was walking home with Ruby, who was at the same school, in Year Three.

"So . . . you're enjoying it?" said Ruby. "Y'know. Having your birthday every day . . . ?"

"Of course!"

Sam thought this was a weird question. He'd told Ruby about the Silly Words lesson. Today, they'd done a whole class on Who Can Blow The Loudest

Raspberry (strangely enough, Mr Barrington, as it turned out). And then a final session on the Stupidest Food (a tie between Cheese Bananas and Cat-food Crumble).

"It's not getting at all . . . boring . . . ?"

"No!" said Sam.

"Because when we get home Mum and Dad will have made a cake and party food and stuff. And they'll have organised some treat, like they did yesterday and the day before . . . What did they do again . . . ?"

"Oh! It was great!" said Sam. "They . . ." He paused. "We . . ."

That was weird. He couldn't remember.

". . . had pizza!" he said. "We went out and had pizza, and then we went to the late-night showing at the Planetarium. It was fun!"

Ruby shook her head. "No, actually, Sam. That was three days ago. Yesterday we went to the zoo!"

She gave him a look as she said it. A look Sam didn't like one bit.

"What are you saying?" said Sam.

"Nothing," said Ruby.

"You are. You're trying to spoil everything. Which is a horrible thing to do . . . on my *birthday*!"

Ruby nodded, and seemed to sigh. "OK. Sorry!" she said, and skipped off ahead.

Despite Sam's refusal to think about what Ruby was saying – he knew it was something troubling, but he couldn't quite say what it was – he did make an unusual decision as he walked home behind his skipping sister. Which was, a few minutes later, not to go straight home. He suggested to Ruby, because it was on their way home, that instead they should pop in to where their grandparents lived.

His grandparents lived in a place called Abbey Court, which was a building that provided something called "sheltered accommodation". This meant that it was a place where old people could live and have some help, but not actually an old-age home. It wasn't, to be honest, somewhere that Sam usually wanted to go, but – apart from wanting to make it clear to Ruby that she wasn't always the good one – something about what she'd said had made him not want to rush home and get the cake and the party food and the treat straight away, like he normally would. Something about it had made him want to put off the next birthday moment for a little while.

Plus, perhaps Grandpa Sam would say some of his funny swearwords.

They went in through the front gate, and up to the lobby with Abbey Court written on it. As Sam opened one of the glass doors, he thought again about how strange it was that he wanted to put off going home and having more birthday-time, more birthday-ness. He thought that was very odd. He also thought it was odd that it was so dark in the lobby. It was normally quite brightly lit.

Then, suddenly, the lights went on! To reveal Sam's grandparents and everyone else who lived at Abbey Court standing there in party hats, blowing party horns. Grandma Glenda and Grandma Poppy were holding a cake between them. It had a model of Abbey Court on it, including the sign – SHELTERED ACCOMMODATION – in green icing. They were holding it in a slightly uncomfortable diagonal way, as Poppy was a lot taller than Glenda. The model of Abbey Court was, in fact, sliding dangerously towards Glenda.

"Happy birthday, Sam!" said the residents of Abbey Court. Not entirely together, as some of them got his name wrong – one said Sammy, another Samantha and one, Dick – but it was still an amazing thing to see.

And then, even more amazing: each resident
of Abbey Court came up to Sam with individually
wrapped presents. Some of these wouldn't, it has to
be said, have been on any of Sam's birthday lists – a
packet of Werther's Originals, some shoelaces, a jar
of polish called Duraglit and something else that
turned out to be a case for false teeth – but
he said, "Thank you!" as he unwrapped
every one.

Each of the residents said, "It's a pleasure!" and, "Don't worry about sending a thank-you card!" before wandering back into the main building.

"But . . ." said Sam, "but . . . how did you know I was coming?"

"I'm not sure!" said Grandpa Mike. "It was you, wasn't it, Glenda? You said Sam would probably pop in today! Didn't you?"

"Oh, typical!" said Grandma Poppy. "It had to be *your* side of the family that knew! Of course!"

"Don't be so stupid!" said Grandma Glenda. "Why shouldn't it be?"

"Yes!" said Grandpa Mike. "After all, it wasn't gonna be Grandpa Sam, was it? 'E wouldn't have known. Because 'e doesn't *know* anythin' any more!"

Sam frowned. It was at that point that he realised that Grandpa Sam hadn't been there. At all. During the whole party. And he still wasn't there now. Where was he?

"Grandpa Mike! Grandma Glenda! Grandma Poppy!"

They all stopped and looked round. It was Ruby who had spoken.

"Remember: it's Sam's *birthday*. Isn't it?"

"Oh yes."

"Oh yes."

"Oh yes," the three of them said. And then they

looked at each other and did a very bad attempt at smiling. At each other.

Sam looked at them. "Um . . ." he said. "Where's Grandpa Sam?"

They all turned to each other. Grandma Poppy frowned. "I don't know," she said. "He was here at lunch . . ."

"Oh no," said Grandpa Mike. "The old codger's done a runner."

CHAPTER 13
IT ALWAYS JUST POINTS STRAIGHT BACK AT ME

But at that moment the doors of the lobby opened again.

"By the beard of Drayton Park! Noam Billybags! What the pluperfect naughty aches are you lot all doing down here?"

It was Grandpa Sam, coming through the door, led by Carmel, a nice lady who worked at Abbey Court.

"Found him by the bus stop! Said he was going to

the countryside for the weekend!" she said, laughing.

"I don't get out enough at this place," said Grandpa Sam. "I like being outside. I used to be in the Boy Scouts, y'know!"

"I know, Grandpa," said Sam. "You told me all about it once. About the knots and the uniform and the tents and learning Morse code and everything!"

"Sam!" he said. "How raspberringly mordacious it is to see you!"

And opened his arms. Sam ran in and gave him a hug.

"I see you're wearing that watch I gave you!"

This was true. When Sam had set out for school that morning, he'd put on the old watch, for the first time, in fact, since he'd got it. Perhaps subconsciously, he'd already been planning to pop in to Abbey Court and see his grandpa – who he knew would be pleased he was wearing it.

"Keeps fabulous time, that one! It was my dad's!"

"Was it?" said Sam.

"Oh yes."

Sam looked at the watch with new eyes. It was nice, in an old-stuff kind of way. The strap was all brown and leathery – a bit like Grandpa Sam's skin, although not quite as pockmarked – and the face of the watch was gold and white. He could see that even though it was old, Grandpa Sam was right that it worked: the second hand was gliding smoothly round the numbers with no sign of hesitation.

He decided he might wear it every day, after all.

"Hey!" said Grandpa Sam, spotting Glenda and Poppy, still holding the cake. The model of Abbey Court had now slid on to Glenda's hands. She was of course refusing to lick off the icing. "What a shambozlingly terrible idea for a cake! What's going on?"

"It's Sam's birthday, you silly old fool!" said Grandpa Mike.

"Is it?"

Sam nodded.

"But Sam's birthday is the eighth of September. Is today the eighth of September?"

There was a pause while everyone frowned.

"Well . . ." said Sam, "no . . . but . . ."

"I don't remember much," said Grandpa Sam, rubbing Sam's hair. "But I always remember that, don't I? Eighth of September: Sam's birthday! I was the first person to visit him in hospital, you know."

"Yeah, yeah," said Grandpa Mike. "And you never let us forget it neither."

"But *he has* forgotten . . ." whispered Grandma Glenda, bending down towards Sam's ear. "About your birthday being every day now. Never mind. *We* all know."

"Oh well. If we are all giving you *more* presents, here!" said Grandpa Sam. "Have this too!"

He rummaged in his pocket, and then took out a

small battered-looking leather case. It looked really old, like something from the First World War. He handed it to Sam.

"What's that?" said Sam.

"It's a compass I've had from when I was in the Scouts. I was using it to find my way to the country."

"Yes," said Carmel, patting Grandpa Sam on the back, "Good if you *do* keep that, Sam. It might be better if

your grandpa *didn't* have something with an arrow on it pointing the way out of here . . ."

"Ha!" said Grandpa Sam. "If only. That arrow's wonky. It always just points straight back at me! Follows me all over the place!"

"Yes, well, anyway!" said Carmel, waving all the residents back towards the inner door of the lobby. "Party's over, I'm afraid!"

CHAPTER 14
CAN'T MAKE OUT WHAT YOU'RE SAYING THERE AT ALL

S am kept going to school on schooldays. But that
didn't mean that his parents stopped celebrating
his birthday at home. They changed some things
around – for example, on September the fourteenth,
Vicky swapped his breakfast doughnut for Sam's
second favourite, French toast and Nutella – and
from the fifteenth his presents – which on that day
were a NERF gun, a metal detector and a basketball
– started to come not from his dad nipping out

quickly to the shops but from the internet – but otherwise it was always birthday business as usual.

On September the sixteenth, while Sam was at school, though – and Charlie was on his laptop scrolling through some shopping pages to try to find some presents for the *next* few days – Vicky said to Sam's dad:

"Charlie?"

They were in the kitchen. He was at the table, and she was baking, of course, a cake. A football cake. Sam didn't like football that much, but she was starting to struggle for birthday themes.

"Do you think Sam would like a knight's outfit?" Sam's dad asked. "You know, with a helmet, and a tunic and—"

"Charlie. I'm a bit worried."

Charlie turned away from the computer.

"About what?"

Vicky came over, dusting her hands. "Well. About

how we're going to – you know – afford all this . . . ?"

Charlie nodded. "Yes. I'm a bit worried about that too."

"Because it is his birthday every day now . . ."

"Yes."

"And so we're spending a lot of money on him every day . . ."

"Yes."

"And we don't have that much . . ."

"Yes."

There was a pause while both of them looked at each other blankly.

Because, it seemed, as a result of Sam's wish, a world had arisen in which the idea that his birthday could *not* be every day was impossible to imagine, or understand. If someone had turned up at the flat with an enormous placard reading, "IT WOULD MAKE YOUR LIFE MUCH EASIER IF SAM'S BIRTHDAY WAS ONLY ONCE A YEAR. HEY, WHAT

ABOUT MAKING IT . . . JUST AN IDEA . . . THE DAY HE WAS BORN?" his parents would have looked up at that placard, shaken their heads and gone:

Nope. Can't make out what you're saying there at all.

Which perhaps explains why, at the end of that blank pause, and with Vicky still looking worried, Charlie just turned back to his computer, on the page for the knight's tunic and helmet, and clicked BUY.

PART 2

FOR HE'S A JOLLY GOOD FELLOW . . .

So this went on ALL YEAR. I can't describe to you every single birthday Sam had – well I could, but the book would be very big, and might fall painfully on your toe – so let me give you some of that year's highlights: Sam's best birthday bits.

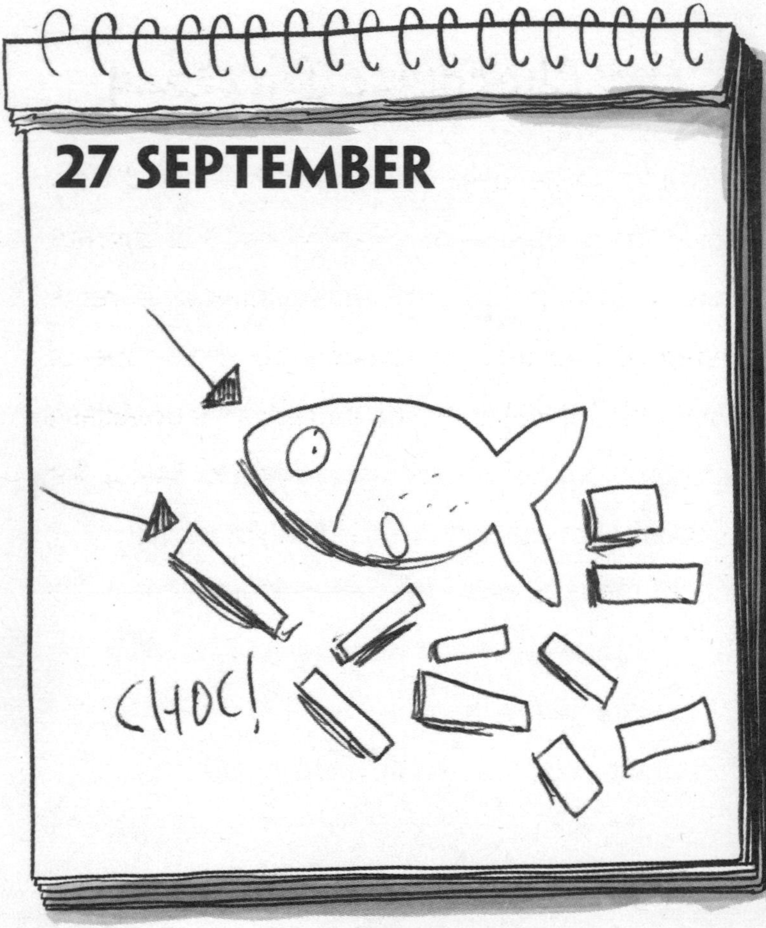
27 SEPTEMBER
CHOC!

The Chocolate Birthday

Knowing that he loved chocolate, Charlie and Vicky decided Sam was allowed to eat chocolate all day. But it wasn't going to be just bars. Instead his parents melted and shaped chocolate into the shape of other food: chocolate bacon and eggs for breakfast, chocolate burger (including chocolate buns) for lunch, and chocolate fish and chips for dinner.

13 OCTOBER

Spock's-birthday Birthday

Sam asked for this birthday to also be Spock's (even though it's unlikely the guinea pig had been born on this day: then again, we know that isn't a vital feature for birthdays at the moment). So Spock got a special breakfast (not a doughnut, or chocolate bacon and eggs, but a very neatly whirled piece of carrot and some lettuce cut like roses). He got presents, which Sam unwrapped for him. These were: a swinging ball, a wheel, which he didn't use: he glared at it with quite a strong sense of, "Am I a hamster? Well, am I?"; and another carrot. He seemed to like this last present best.

31 OCTOBER

The Halloween Birthday

On this day, Sam's birthday had to be frightening, obviously. So his birthday breakfast included a blood drink (blackcurrant juice) and cut-off fingers (sausages with dobs of tomato sauce). His cake was in the shape of a skull. His party – because he had at least one every day, as we know – involved everyone coming as monsters. And when he went trick-or-treating later on (as the Grim Reaper) everyone in the street made sure to give him the best sweets in their buckets, and say "Happy birthday!" as well as "Happy Halloween!"

5 NOVEMBER

The Guy Fawkes Birthday

Sort of like the Halloween Birthday, but with fireworks instead of frightening stuff. They had a birthday cake with a little Catherine wheel and a little Guy, with golden flame-like icing underneath him. (Vicky was quite pleased about these topical birthdays, the ones that went with other dates, as it meant she had a new theme . . .) In the evening, they had their own fireworks party. Charlie hired – it cost quite a lot – a man to create a display that said, "Happy birthday, Sam!" in the sky

20 NOVEMBER

The Skateboarding Birthday

You've guessed the theme here, obviously. So, yes –
Sam had a skateboard cake (the whole thing in the

shape of a board, with icing-sugar silver wheels), and his party was in the bowl underneath Noam Chomsky House! His parents had the whole area decked out with lights, and there was music, and all Sam's friends from school who could skate brought their boards, and had a brilliant time.

The only shame was that Zada, whom Sam had not seen since that first – well, second – birthday evening, didn't come, even though Sam had put an invitation through the door of every flat on the fifteenth floor in the hope that one of them would reach her.

Sam really wanted Zada to see how much better he'd got at skateboarding through practising all the things she'd taught him since that evening they'd first met. But she never came.

25 DECEMBER

The Christmas Birthday

Ruby had been worried about this for some time. How would Sam's birthday work, being on the same day as Christmas? Charlie and Vicky explained that there were a lot of people who did have their birthdays on Christmas Day, but Ruby – who, let's not forget, was very clever – explained that that was all very well, but those people were used to it. From the day they were born. They didn't have to suddenly get used to it, out of nowhere, *this* Christmas.

So what they did was split the day. They had Christmas in the morning – so that all the presents, Santa's and the ones under the tree, could be given out, and they took Christmas all the way up, in fact, to lunchtime – and then after lunch it became Sam's birthday again. Which meant the grandparents staying all day.

This worked out all right – and in a way was quite good, as the best part of Christmas *is* the morning: once the Queen comes on the telly, as Charlie said, it's sort of all over – plus it did mean an extra burst of presents (well, for Sam, at least). But it did also mean a lot more eating. You try having turkey and roast potatoes and Christmas pudding, and then a cake at teatime.

31 DECEMBER

The New Year's Eve Birthday

Same kind of issue here. Although at least they didn't have to double up on presents. But Charlie and Vicky did always allow the children to stay up till midnight on New Year's Eve. In fact, they always did a secret thing, which was to go up to the roof of Noam Chomsky House. You weren't really allowed there, but because Charlie sometimes did some DIY work for the people who ran the tower block, he had been given a key to the roof area.

It had been snowing. And it seemed, as the Green family went out on to the roof, to have been snowing more on the top of Noam Chomsky House than anywhere else, as if it was a mountain that was so high the weather was colder on the top of it. Noam Chomsky House was not a beautiful place, but here on the roof at midnight on New Year's Eve it was a beautiful place to be. Beneath them, the snow crunched underfoot, and the lights of the city twinkled everywhere, reflecting, it seemed, the bright stars – and then, when the clock struck midnight, fireworks went off all around them! They had the best seat in the whole city to watch the colours fill the night sky!

As the fireworks exploded, they toasted the New Year – Charlie and Vicky with champagne, and Ruby and Sam with sparkling apple juice – and also Sam's birthday. Because, obviously, at one second past midnight, it was *another* birthday, as the next day, and the New Year, came in.

25 FEBRUARY

The Samuelus9 Birthday

On this one, Charlie and Vicky made the whole flat look like a made-up planet, called Samuelus9. On Samuelus9, all the light was green – they did this by taking out the normal light bulbs, and replacing them with green ones – and all the food was blue – using blue food dye. Charlie had built, in the kitchen, a viewing station through which you could see Samuelolis, the huge city in the middle of Samuelus9 (a big backcloth, made by Vicky, using some sci-fi images from the internet).

Vicky had also made a little Spock – as in Mr Spock – outfit for Spock. This was a uniform, with no buttons. The guinea pig wore it with quite a strong sense of, "I'm not even going to make my face say anything about this."

Sam got a voice-changer for a present that day. You know, one of those megaphone things that changes your voice in lots of ways, making it sound really low or really high or like a frightening robot. Sam used it to create a high, wobbly alien voice in which he spoke all day.

Sam's friends came to the party dressed as made-up citizens of Samuelus9. The specifics of this were left up to them. Barry Bennett looked great as a completely green astronaut, and Fred and Ellie as twin orcs, but Morris Fawcett had misunderstood and come as a tube of skin lotion. Called Samuelus9.

17 MARCH

The Sugar-free Birthday

This was one that Sam felt he should do in order to be healthier. It didn't work. It was the only birthday idea to be abandoned halfway through.

22 MAY

The Running-out-of-ideas-tell-you-what-let's-do-as-much-of-the-day-as-we-can-standing-on-one-leg Birthday

I think the title of that birthday kind of . . . tells you all you need to know.

3 JUNE

Ruby's-birthday Birthday

This was quite an awkward one. Ruby had, in fact, gone to her parents a month before, and said:

"Mum? Dad? What about my birthday?"

"What do you mean, love?" said Vicky.

"Well . . . it will be my birthday in a month. And, of course, it's going to be Sam's birthday every day up until then. And *on* then. *On* my birthday."

"Well, of course," said Vicky. "Of course it will also be Sam's birthday."

"Yes," said Ruby "Yes, but . . . will we have enough money left by then to get presents for . . . people in this family . . . ?"

"Oh, I'm sure we will!" said Vicky, not entirely convincingly.

"Yes!" said Charlie. Even less convincingly.

"And will it . . ." said Ruby, with a hint of sadness, ". . . will it still be a special day? Do you think?" And then, not quite as throwaway as she normally said it – more, as if it really meant something this time – "Actually?"

Vicky and Charlie opened their mouths to say,

"Of course!" and, "Yes!" and, "Why ever not!" – all the things you would expect – but, strangely, nothing came out. Neither of them could quite promise that.

As it was, it worked out not too badly. They didn't split the day like Christmas – too worried about which child might have felt favourited by being first. Two cakes, two sets of presents, two parties. Ruby did feel it was a special day for her.

Maybe not *quite* as special as if Sam hadn't been having his birthday. But still . . . special.

Also, Ruby *didn't* get a kitten. She hadn't been expecting it, not really – especially not at the moment, with how difficult it was with money – but still a part of her had been hoping that the day might have started with a trip to the pet shop, and a series of sweet, sad kitten eyes looking up at her, saying, with those eyes, "Pick me, Ruby, pick me!"

But no. Instead she got some nice toys, and three books about science (remember, she was very clever, and did genuinely *like* science). And Sam gave Ruby a lovely present. OK, it was one of *his* presents – a DVD of a movie called *Galaxy Quest* – but Ruby was very happy with it. At least it meant that Charlie and Vicky didn't have to buy an extra present for Sam to give Ruby. Because Ruby wasn't wrong about how much Sam's birthdays were costing them.

Actually.

The Grandparents-organise-
it-all Birthday

Yes: Grandma Poppy, Grandma Glenda, Grandpa
Mike and Grandpa Sam took on the responsibility

of Sam's birthday for one day. They felt it was time to give Charlie and Vicky a day off.

Which was a nice idea. It had its problems, though. Grandma Glenda brought in the birthday breakfast-in-bed tray in the morning, but, because she was fairly shaky on her legs, ended up spilling most of it over Spock. Poppy made a cake, which looked very tasty, but she coughed a lot after lighting the candles and blew them out. Which put Sam off it a bit.

Poppy ate it, of course. Glenda didn't have any because, she said, "It'll go straight to my hips," and Poppy said, "Well, it'll have company," and then there was a bit of arguing until Vicky reminded them that it was of course Sam's birthday.

Mike was in charge of the treat, which was going to the cinema, but he drove there so slowly in his extremely old car with a wooden back half that by the time they got there the film was halfway through. Sam didn't really mind, though, seeing as it was in black and white and called *Whoops, Matron, Don't Mind If I Do!*, so they went for a burger instead, which was great.

It was only when they got home that they realised Grandpa Sam hadn't come with them. Vicky and Charlie didn't know where he was either. Everyone was worried that he might have walked out of the house and gone missing, but then they found him in Sam's room, playing with all the toys. When they opened the bedroom door, he was wearing the knight's helmet and tunic, and brandishing a lightsaber.

"Gadshmooking blunderbusses!" Grandpa Sam shouted. "There's a treasure trove of stuff in here! Ha! Ha! Ha!" And he poked at them with the lightsaber as if he was a knight guarding the entrance to a castle.

It took them quite a long time to get Grandpa Sam out of that stuff and back downstairs. On his birthday list for this one, Sam had originally asked that all the grandparents stay and have a sleepover – perhaps with a midnight feast as well – but after that he decided it might be better if they all went home.

"Bye, Sam," they said. "Happy birthday!"

Or most of them did.

"What?" said Grandpa Sam. "Sam's birthday is the eighth of September. I always remember that."

They got into the lift.

"Let me explain again…" said Poppy. "Sam has his birthday every day n—"

The lift doors closed.

20 JULY

The End-of-term Birthday

It was the end of term at Bracket Wood. And because Sam was in Year Six it was actually his last day at the school. In the morning they had their Leaving Assembly!

So Year Six did all the normal stuff that happens at a Leaving Assembly – singing songs, reciting poems, telling stories about their time at Bracket Wood and putting up with a *lot* of parental crying – but then at the end they also sang "Happy Birthday" to Sam. In fact, they sang a slightly different version of it than usual, which went:

"Happy birthday to you,
Happy birthday to you,
Happy birthday, dear Sa-am . . ."

And then, on the same note as *Sa-am*:

"Thank goodness it's the last time!

We've done this every day for a year,

Except the holidays, of course,

I mean we don't mind . . ."

("Well, I do!" said Morris Fawcett.)

"But great that this is

the last time . . ."

As I say, all on one note. Musically, it was a tad experimental, to be honest, for a Leaving Assembly (particularly as they'd just done "Red And Yellow And Pink And Green").

And then:

"Happy birthday to you!!"

1 AUGUST

TREE
HOUSE

The Outdoors Birthday

Sam, inspired partly by his Grandpa Sam's love of the great outdoors, had a party in a nearby forest. All his friends came, and they had a competition building treehouses (Charlie was pleased about this one, as he was able to pick up all the wood and nails from HomeFront). Once it was finished, Sam's family and all his friends climbed up to their treehouses and had picnic food, and, of course, cake. From here, they could see over the city.

They stayed there for ages, right into the evening. As the lights started to go down, Sam, feeling very happy, looked to his left, where he could see the little island on the river, the one that was visible from their seventeenth-floor flat.

PART 3

FOR HE'S A JOLLY—
OH.

That, sadly, was the last really nice birthday they had for a while. After that, things started to go a bit wrong. Turn the page to see just how wrong.

CHAPTER 15
TOO MUCH

You see?

Sam had become very, very large. From too much special breakfast. And too much cake. His room had got too crowded because of too many presents. Spock had not seen daylight for some time because the knight's helmet and tunic had been lying on top of his cage since Vicky had gently removed them from Grandpa Sam.

And Sam hadn't just changed physically. He'd changed as a person. He'd stopped writing thank-you notes (to be fair, he'd had to write a *lot* of them). He'd stopped even *saying* thank you when he got presents. He'd started demanding bigger and bigger cakes, and more and more exciting parties.

Meanwhile, for the rest of the family, things had got considerably *less* lavish. Since halfway through the year, Charlie and Vicky (and Ruby) had been eating mainly baked beans on toast. For almost every meal. And now, further on in the year, they just never went out (except to take Sam, of course, to the cinema, or the swimming pool, or a climbing rock, or paintballing, or wherever, on his birthdays).

On Charlie and Vicky's own birthdays, they hadn't given each other any presents except cards, which they'd made themselves. And they never read anything any more – they used to devour books, and newspapers together – except, it seemed, credit card bills.

Then on the third of September, this happened.

CHAPTER 16
YOU'LL WHAT?

I 've told you," said Sam, spitting out his doughnut, "I don't *want* that any more."

Vicky looked on nervously. Whereas Sam had got fat, his mum had got thin. But not in any kind of healthy way. She looked like a rake.

Sam was sitting up in bed. Charlie had made him a special tray, fitted to his bed-frame, which made it easier for him to have breakfast in bed served to him every morning. Vicky had brought in the classic special breakfast, the doughnuts and the lemonade and the bacon, sausages, eggs and beans.

"I know you said that, darling," said Vicky. "But I've run out of ideas . . ."

"And these aren't even the *nice* doughnuts. From the bakery. These are . . ." Sam looked underneath the bun, where a brand name was embossed in the sugar. "Urrrgh! Supermarket doughnuts!"

"I'm sorry, Sammy! But we can't afford the bakery doughnuts any more!"

"Anyway, Sam!" said Charlie, taking the tray away. "Why don't you open your presents?"

Yawning, and raising his eyes to the heavens, Sam said: "Why don't you open them? I can't be bothered."

Charlie frowned and, for a second, seemed to have to control himself. But then he said: "Fine. Yes. All right." He undid the ribbon, and took off the wrapping from the first one. Which was a chess set.

"Hmm," said Sam. "I suppose I could learn."

"You said you wanted to . . . ?"

"Did I? I can't remember. Next!"

"OK, just give me a minute . . ." Charlie handed him another present. It was a book: *Caring for Guinea Pigs*.

Sam looked at it for a second, but then tossed it away, saying, "Yes, well, that's really a present for Spock, isn't it? And we already did his birthday a while back. Give it to Ruby. She basically looks after him now anyway."

"Only because *you* don't," said Ruby, coming into the room.

"No," said Sam. "Because guinea pigs are for babies. And you're a baby."

Charlie looked even more like he was having to control himself now. He went very red, as if holding his breath.

Sam didn't seem to notice, just looked up and

held out his hands for his third present.

"Here it is!" said Vicky quickly, interposing herself between Sam and his dad.

Sam held the present in his hands, turning it over.

"What's this?" asked Sam.

"Binoculars!" said Vicky.

Sam paused, turning them again. "Well, what's the point of that? I've got a telescope."

"Sam . . ." said his dad, his voice brimming with anger. "Don't speak to your mum like that."

"Well, I have. And I don't even use *that* much now. You can't see anything through it anyway. Just basically your own eyelashes."

"Sam . . ."

"And I'm not really interested in sci-fi or space any more."

"*What?*"

"I'm not. I was for a bit. But that's a thing parents do, isn't it? They decide, 'Oh yes, our son likes x –

that's his thing,' because he *once* said he did, so for every birthday and Christmas after that they get him stuff to do with x, because that's *easy*."

And with that he tossed the binoculars away, just like he had the book about guinea pigs.

But he tossed the binoculars away more forcefully than the book about guinea pigs. Partly because they were heavier, so it took a little more force, and partly because he wanted to make a point more than he did with the other toss. It was more of a throw, in fact, than a toss. And it was in the direction of the telescope. Again, to make his point.

The binoculars twirled in a little arc across the room. It did seem for most of their journey in the air that no greater harm would come to them, or anything else, than falling on the floor, unbroken.

But strangely, at the last moment of the arc, the binoculars seemed to get a second wind – maybe it was *actually* a second wind, as Sam's window was ever so slightly open – and they lifted higher than expected . . . before coming down, fast, on top of the telescope.

These binoculars were really quite heavy, as we know. Binoculars generally are (lift some, if you get the chance). A telescope, though in some sense the big brother of binoculars, is lighter of frame, and more delicately constructed. Which became clear when Sam's smashed into many different pieces.

"Oh no!" screamed Vicky, running over to the mess.

"Samuel!" shouted Sam's dad. Which was something he hardly ever called him. Only when he was really, really cross. For a second, Sam looked genuinely sorry, and genuinely scared. "I've just about had

enough of this!" continued Charlie. "If you don't stop behaving so badly, I'll . . ."

But then Sam's face changed. To something less scared, less sorry.

"You'll . . . *what*?" he said.

"I'll . . ." said Charlie.

"What will you do?"

"I'll . . ." Charlie looked at Vicky, who was trying, uselessly, to pick up the fragments of telescope and binoculars. Sam's dad knew, or had an inkling at least, what was coming: what had clearly occurred to Sam he could always say. Or, to put it another way, what he could now say, always.

"Yes?" said Sam.

"I'll make you very sorry!" shouted Charlie despairingly.

"But, Dad . . ." said Sam, smiling a little . . . I'm afraid there's no other way to put this . . . evilly. "It's my *birthday*."

CHAPTER 17
FEELING A BIT LOW

Sam spent most of the next day locked in his room. His room hadn't had a lock before, but he'd asked for one on his birthday list a few days earlier and his dad had fixed it up for him.

"Is this a good idea?" asked Vicky while Charlie was screwing in the plates. "I have a bad feeling about it."

"Who knows?" said Charlie, shrugging. "But, to be honest, after his behaviour yesterday, I wouldn't mind *not* seeing him for a little while."

It led to an odd day. As usual, Sam's parents brought him his special breakfast – with bakery-sourced doughnuts – and presents: a Rubik's cube, a laser keyring, a pair of gloves (they were trying to keep the presents small, as there was no space left in Sam's room for anything big, plus it was a bit cheaper). But when they knocked on the door there was no response, so they just left the presents outside on a tray.

Some time later, when they came back to check, the food and presents were gone, and the empty tray had been left outside the door.

They had a party planned that day: a rock-star party. All of Sam's friends from his old school turned up dressed as various musical superstars – Barry Bennett was Justin Bieber; Fred and Ellie Stone were Jedward; Malcolm Bailey was, for some reason, Benny out of Abba; and Morris Fawcett got it wrong

and came as Simon Cowell –
haircut, big trousers, everything
– but Sam wouldn't come out of
his room, so they all had to
go away.

Which left Charlie and
Vicky and Ruby sitting
around in the living room
afterwards, feeling a bit low, and
not really knowing what to say
or do.

"I miss the old Sam,"
said Ruby.

"Actually," said Charlie, "so do I."

And then the phone rang.

CHAPTER 18
SIR GUINEA PIG AND THE GREEN KNIGHT

A few minutes later, there was a knock on Sam's door.

"Go away!" said Sam, from inside.

There was a short pause.

"*Unless* you've got some presents."

"No!" said Ruby.

"Oh, it's *you*," said Sam. "What do you want?"

"Can I come in, please?"

"No!"

"Why not?"

There was a longer pause from inside. The truth was that Sam didn't really know why he'd shut himself in his room. It was some sort of reaction to the telescope breaking, but he didn't know exactly what it was. But before he could think of an answer to Ruby's question he heard her say:

"Aren't you . . . lonely? In there all by yourself?"

"No!" he said back with some emphasis, it suddenly coming to him what to say. "I'm not. Because I've got all my presents and toys to play with!"

He settled back smugly on his inflatable chair (a present from the sixth of October last year), put his feet up on a train-set box (present from the third of November) and drank some leftover lemonade from his cup with S on it (present from the fourth of May).

That's told her, he thought.

Then he had an idea. He'd get the voice-changer

from his Samuelus9 birthday and use it to make his voice really deep and then roar through the door.

That'll scare her off, he thought.

Only he couldn't find the voice-changer anywhere. He scrabbled around in his presents. *I'm sure it was here somewhere*, he thought. But no, nowhere to be seen.

OK, he thought, *I've got a really high-powered torch somewhere. Super-bright 8,000 lumens* (present from the second of March)! *I'll find that instead, open the door quickly and shine that in her face!* That'll *scare her off*, he thought.

Only he couldn't find that, either. *What's going on?* he wondered. But it *was* very messy in there.

"Right," he heard Ruby say. "Well . . . *that* – having all your presents and toys to play with by yourself – still sounds a bit . . . lonely to me. Actually."

Sam looked over at his door, with its poster of the solar system on it, a present from the twenty-ninth of September – *I must remember to take that down*, he thought in passing, *to make the point about how I don't really like space any more.*

"Listen . . ." he said, coming over and speaking right into the door. "You're just jealous. Because it's not *your* birthday every day!"

"Yes, I am," said Ruby simply. Which took the wind out of Sam's sails, as he was expecting her to deny it. "*Very* jealous. But not *just* jealous. I've got some vegetables for Spock. Or do you want him to starve?"

Sam glanced over. He could see Spock looking up at him through the visor of the knight's helmet, with quite a strong sense of, "Who am I? Sir Guinea Pig and the Green Knight?"

Reluctantly, he turned the key in the lock and opened the door.

"Happy birthday," said Ruby, not very enthusiastically, when she came in.

Sam nodded and turned away. As he began to shut his door, he heard the front door slam.

"Who's that going out?" he said. "Is it one of my school friends who came for the rock-star party? Did one of them stay?"

Sam sounded, even though he didn't really want to, hopeful.

Ruby shook her head. She was bending down and clearing off the knight costume from Spock's cage. Spock looked up at her with quite a strong sense of, "About time . . ."

"No," she said. "They all left. They couldn't wait for you any longer. They've gone to play football."

"Oh . . ." said Sam. He went over to his window and looked out. He could see Charlie getting into the family car.

"Where's Dad going? Out to get me some more presents?"

"No," said Ruby plainly. "He's going to look for Grandpa Sam."

Sam looked round at her sharply. "What do you mean, look for Grandpa Sam? Going to Abbey Court?"

"No," said Ruby. "You see . . . Grandpa Sam's not there."

CHAPTER 19
NOBODY KNOWS

Sam left the window and crouched down next to her, by Spock's cage. Spock glanced at him – in between munches of lettuce – with quite a strong sense of, "Oh, hello: nice to see *you* again, I'm sure . . . For babies, am I?"

Sam gave him a look back that said, "Sorry."

Then he turned to Ruby.

"Well, where is Grandpa, then?"

"Nobody knows."

Sam frowned. "What do you mean, 'nobody knows'?"

"He's gone missing," said Ruby, shutting the little gate in the cage, and standing up. "Like he did before. Only this time he hasn't come back. Abbey Court just phoned to tell us."

Sam stood up too. "Well, he will. Soon. Won't he?"

Ruby shrugged. She turned to go.

"No, wait a minute." She turned round. "Grandpa Sam *will* come back soon. *Won't* he?"

"Er . . ." said Ruby. "I don't think saying it again with slightly more emphasis on certain words changes anything."

"No . . . but . . . but . . ." said Sam, his face contorting a little, on the brink of tears. "I don't *want* him to be missing."

Ruby looked at him. "Neither do I. But he is."

Sam stared at her. "But . . ." he said, one tear now coming out of each eye. "But . . ."

"Yes?"

". . . it's my *birthday*!" he said, sobbing now, properly.

At which point, Vicky, having heard the conversation from the living room, came in and hugged him (with a little difficulty: there was more of him to hug than before). And said, patting him gently on the back:

"Yes . . . I'm sorry, Sam. I don't think . . . in this particular case . . . that that will make any difference."

CHAPTER 20
NEVER MIND

When Sam's dad came back about an hour later, Sam burst out of his room and ran down the hall. Which left him out of breath, since he was, as we know, carrying more weight than usual.

"Dad! Dad! Did you find him?"

Charlie shook his head. He looked at Vicky. "I drove all round the houses. No sign."

"What did they say at Abbey Court?"

"Carmel said they've spoken to the local police. And they said they'll let us know . . . if they find him."

"If!" said Sam. "Dad! What do you mean *if*?"

"Sorry, Sam. When, I mean. *When* they find him."

Sam glanced at Ruby, who was starting to look very upset too.

"But why are you here?" asked Sam. "Carry on looking! Please, Dad! He might just have been asleep under a bench somewhere when you drove past and now he's woken up and doesn't remember where he is and—"

"Well, I would, Sam," said Charlie, "but I had to come home."

"*Why?*"

"Because," said Vicky, "we have to get stuff ready for your birthday."

"Yes. There's cake to be shared, and later we're going out for fish and chips," said Charlie.

"Yes! Sorry it's not burgers this time, Sam, but you did put fish and chips down on one of your" – Vicky started pointing at the rows of paper on the

wall – "birthday special-treats-on-the-day lists . . .
this one, I think—"

"And I have to buy some presents for tomorrow!"
said Charlie. "Thank the Lord for next-day delivery,
that's all I can say—"

"Dad!" said Sam, interrupting him. "Never mind
my birthday!"

Charlie frowned. Vicky frowned. Ruby frowned.

"Sorry, Sam," replied Charlie. "What did you say?"

Sam took a deep breath. He could hardly believe
he was saying it himself. Certainly not for a second
time.

"I said: NEVER MIND MY BIRTHDAY!"

His family kept on frowning. Then, Charlie shook his head.

"Sorry, Sam. I don't understand."

"What don't you understand? I'm saying – until we find Grandpa Sam – *let's forget about my birthday! Don't worry about my birthday! We can do without my birthday!*"

Charlie turned to Vicky.

"Can you make out what he's saying?"

Vicky shook her head. "Doesn't sound like anything to me . . ."

"What about you, Ruby?"

"All I could hear was the word 'birthday', over and over again . . ." said Ruby.

"Oh right. Yes!" said Charlie. "Don't worry! Whatever happens with Grandpa Sam, we will make sure we don't forget about your birthday. Or birthdays, rather!"

"Yes! They'll keep going, of course!"

"But, Mum, Dad . . . that's exactly what I *wasn't* saying!" said Sam.

"What was?" asked Vicky.

"Yes, what was?" asked Charlie.

"That I want my birthdays to carry on forever!"

Vicky and Charlie looked at each other.

"Well, good! We'll make sure they do!" said Charlie.

"Now," said Vicky, "who's for cake?"

And with that she went off to the fridge. Sam watched, open-mouthed. And not because he wanted to make it easier for cake to go in there.

CHAPTER 21
ESPECIALLY ON YOUR BIRTHDAY

"Hello," a voice said. "Goodness. I almost didn't recognise you. You have changed very much since I last saw you."

Sam looked up from where he was sitting on a bench near the tower block. He blinked in the glow of the streetlight. He hadn't been outside for some time. After a moment he recognised Zada, holding her battered skateboard.

"Hey, hello!" he said. "Where have you been? Haven't seen you for ages!"

"We had to leave here for a little while and go and stay somewhere else, because we thought we were going to be sent away. But now the government has let us come back."

"Oh, great! Have you been skating?" said Sam.

"Yes, but mainly at night. And you?"

"No . . . I've been a bit busy having birthdays." Sam paused, and frowned. "Wait, why mainly at night?"

"I have to help my mum out during the day," said Zada. "I've got two little brothers. So the only time I get to come here is when it gets dark."

Which, indeed, it was. Really dark. Because Sam had been out for some time, on his own. He had gone out on his skateboard, but because he was considerably heavier than last time he'd used it, that had turned out to be difficult. He hadn't ridden it down the streets so much as wobbled it down them.

So, eventually, he'd picked it up and just walked

about in the local area. For a long time: he'd walked all the way to his school, Bracket Wood, and back again, peering into the windows of houses, checking gardens, even looking into bins. And, of course, he'd walked all around the streets surrounding Abbey Court. This was probably useful in one way, as it may have led to him losing some weight.

"What are you doing out so late anyway?" asked Zada.

"Looking for my grandpa . . ." said Sam. "But I can't find him anywhere."

"Oh. Does he live round here?"

"No. Well, not far. In a sort of home. But he's gone missing . . ."

Zada nodded, a little bit like she wasn't surprised. She looked up at the tower block. The lights in some of the flats were still on, but not in others.

"I haven't seen my grandparents for a long time also," said Zada. "They couldn't come with us. When we left. They said they were too old."

"Oh. What about your dad?"

Zada didn't answer this. She just looked down, and silently twirled the wheels of her skateboard. Sam didn't know what to say. Luckily, she spoke, eventually.

"Especially on your birthday," said Zada.

"Sorry?" said Sam.

"Your grandpa going missing. That must make it worse."

Sam looked at her. "Yeah. I suppose so. I dunno."

"Anyway," said Zada, pushing off on her board, "Happy birthday. For the rest of it. And for tomorrow . . ."

She skated off towards the bowl area, under Noam Chomsky House. Sam watched her go, noticing that the wheels on Zada's battered old home-made board seemed considerably looser on the trucks than last time: one of them really looked as if it was about to fall off.

"Zada!" he called.

Zada stopped and turned.

"Never mind about my birthday!" said Sam. "Forget about my birthday!"

Zada stared at him for a second. "Whatever you wish," she said. And then she skated away.

Sam blinked. *Whatever you wish*, he thought.

CHAPTER 22
A WEIRD WISH

Sam looked around his room, stuffed with presents – loads of them piled up on top of each other, toppling, falling off every available space – and thought: *I don't want any of it*. Make it all go away. *All I want is my grandpa*.

He went over to the window, partly to get away from the endless piles of half-used and mainly discarded gifts. One gift that he *did* feel sad about, though, was his telescope, which still lay there in many pieces from the time he had thrown the binoculars at it. He wanted to use it now. It was the present he'd *really* wanted for his birthday – the first and most important – and now it might help him with his idea.

He picked up one end of the telescope, the bit with the eyepiece on, put it to his eye and looked out of the window. Sam was hoping to see another shooting star. He wanted to wish on it. He had his wish all ready.

I wish my birthday WASN'T every day.

It felt weird, that wish. It was like a wish for something not to be a wish. Like wishing for everything you've ever wanted *not* to come true.

But, nonetheless, he felt it very strongly. That was his wish. He just wanted everyone to stop focusing on his birthday so that they could all team up to look for Grandpa Sam.

Unfortunately, he couldn't see any stars, let

alone any shooting stars. And this wasn't just because he was looking through half a telescope. It was because it was not a clear night. Even the moon was only a little visible behind a big hanging cloud.

He tried saying it anyway:

"I wish my birthday wasn't every day!" he said quietly to the night.

He said again, a bit louder:

"I wish my birthday wasn't every day!"

Then Sam looked round, a little embarrassed. He saw Spock looking at him with quite a strong sense of, "Right. And you really think *that's* going to work?" And also with quite a strong sense of, "*Still* no one has properly moved this plastic knight's helmet off my cage . . ."

Sam looked out of the window again. He wondered if anything had happened. It didn't *feel* as if anything had happened.

He wouldn't know, he supposed, until tomorrow morning.

He would have to wait until then, and see if his mum did her customary knock on his door.

CHAPTER 23

THAT ISLAND IN THE MIDDLE
OF THE RIVER

But he was wrong about that. Because right then she did a knock on his door.

"Hi, Sam" said his mum, coming in. "I thought I heard you say something?"

Sam shook his head.

"Oh, right. Well. Now that I'm here . . ." she added, "I was wondering what had happened to your birthday lists. Only . . . it's getting quite hard to know what to buy for you . . . you know . . . what with your birthday being every day . . . and I'm slightly running out of ideas. And you know when you used to write really long lists? That was very helpful . . ."

OK, Sam thought. *Nothing's happened.*

He sighed and looked out of the window again. But, as he did so, he did see something. In the middle of the river, in the centre of the island, there was a glow. Like someone had switched a light on, and then off.

The star! he thought. *That's definitely where it went, then. It fell out of the sky and landed on that island in the middle of the river.*

"So . . ." continued Sam's mum, hesitantly, aware that some of the time these days Sam didn't really seem to want to speak to anyone, "as I was saying, Sam, your lists, you haven't done one for a week or so . . ."

Sam turned round. Then he frowned.

"My birthday lists . . ." he said, sort of in reply, but really as if he was talking to himself. He was thinking about that island in the river, and the light coming from it.

Then, very suddenly, he crouched down, and started scrabbling madly around on the floor, throwing presents behind him as he went.

"Sam?" said his mum. She looked down at him, and then at Ruby, who had wandered into the room. Ruby shrugged her shoulders, and did a finger-twist round her temple.

But Sam just carried on scrabbling, seemingly unbothered about what happened to his presents. *Bang!* Over his shoulder went one of his many model cars. *Crash!* Over his other shoulder went one of his kites! *Slap!* went Ruby's face as a rubber ball that he'd taken out of the packaging but never actually played with hit her in the face.

"Ow!" she said.

Sam looked round. "Sorry," he said. "Wow. It lights up. Who knew?"

Ruby looked at her mum, rubbing her cheek. "At least he's saying sorry again now," she said.

"Sam," said Vicky, "what are you doing?"

"Here it is!" said Sam, holding up a pen. It was silver, and had a top on it, which he was unscrewing.

"Right. Yes. We gave you that . . . about a month ago, I think . . . ? With a pad to write in . . . ?"

"Yes!" said Sam. "And here *that* is!" He held the pad up with his other hand. Then, using it like a brush a waiter might have to sweep away crumbs, he pushed a whole load of other presents, lying on his table, aside. He sat down, flipped to a page on the pad and started scribbling furiously.

"What's going on . . . ?" mouthed Vicky at Ruby.

"I don't know," mouthed Ruby back. She looked down at Spock, who looked up at her with quite a strong sense of, "Don't ask me. I think he's finally cracked."

"OK!" said Sam, standing up and turning round. He tore the piece of paper off the pad, and, stepping over and around about seven different boxes, came to where his mum and sister were standing. "My birthday list!"

"Oh!" said Vicky, looking down at it. "That's great. Have you thought of some new gadgets? Or video games? Or board games? Or . . ."

She stopped at this point, as obviously it was simpler, to answer this question, just to read the list. Which read:

1. Six large planks of wood.
2. A hammer and some nails.
3. Six coils of rope.
4. A roll of gaffer tape.
5. Two brooms.

"You sure about this, Sam?" she asked.

"Quite sure," he said, looking out of the window towards the river.

CHAPTER 24
WITH GREAT POO-ER

The problem for Sam's mum and dad was not getting hold of these things – they shopped for them the next day, and, by the standards of Sam's usual present-wishes, all of them were fairly cheap and available from HomeFront, where Charlie worked.

The problem wasn't getting all this stuff into Sam's room either, as he had cleared up in there, putting all his other presents into four piles (well, towers, really: there were so many presents he'd had to stack them right up to the ceiling), one in each corner.

The problem was the hammering. It went on all of the next day, and into the night. That was bad in itself, as it was very loud, but particularly bad because the next day was, of course, still Sam's birthday. Which meant that when his parents and Ruby knocked on Sam's door, holding his birthday cake, he didn't let them in – not, this time, because he was being moody and grand and didn't want to come out, but because he couldn't hear them and was concentrating on his mission to get to the falling star and un-wish his wish.

After all, Grandpa Sam was still missing and no one seemed to be doing anything about it. The police were going to speak to them all at Abbey Court to get more information for their enquiry, but not till the following day, they'd told Grandma

Poppy, because they were working on something urgent.

Eventually, not sure what to do, Sam's family lit the candles and sang "Happy Birthday" as loudly as they could outside the door to try to make Sam hear them over his own hammering.

It worked: when they got to the words "DEAR SA-AM!!" – all of them red and raw-throated with the effort of keeping the volume up – the hammering stopped for a second, and he opened the door.

"Oh! Thank you so much!" said Sam.

"HAPPY BIRTHDAY TO YOU!!"

"All right, no need to shout . . ." And he blew the candles out.

"Sam . . . ?" said his dad, peering into the room. He could see the edge of one of the planks, which seemed to have been nailed to one of the others, and secured with a piece of rope. The floor, he noticed, was scattered with drawings, like the ones you have to do in DT, with lots of numbers and measurements on them. "What are you making in there?"

"Oh nothing," said Sam, coming out and closing the door. "Shall we go downstairs and cut the cake? Oh, and, Mum and Dad, here's my birthday list for tomorrow . . ."

He handed over another piece of paper. They looked at it.

"Three *more* skateboards?" said Vicky.

"Yes. They can all be the same model as my other one if you like."

His parents exchanged glances.

"Sam," said his dad. "That will cost quite a . . . lot of money . . ."

"Oh! Right." Sam thought for a bit. "I see . . ." he said, opening his door and going back into the room and shutting it behind him.

His family stood outside it, confused: had he reacted badly again? Would he stay in there for the rest of the day? Then, from inside the room, they heard Sam say:

"Can you open the door, please?"

Ruby looked at her parents, shrugged and turned the handle.

"Slowly!" said Sam.

Ruby frowned. But did as he asked, opening the door more slowly.

To reveal: what appeared to be a shaking tower of presents. A model of the *Star Wars Millennium Falcon* was balanced on a helicopter, which was balanced on a walkie-talkie, which was balanced on a kite, which was balanced on a toy crossbow, which was balanced on a tambourine, which was balanced on a pirate ship, which was balanced on a digital alarm clock, which was balanced on an action figure of Spider-Man, which was balanced on a painting set, which was balanced on three juggling sticks, which were balanced, themselves, on two small hands.

Then, Sam's face appeared round the side of the middle of the tower (at about the level of the pirate ship).

"Hello. I thought, Mum – I don't mean to be ungrateful and thanks to you and everyone else who bought these presents but – I thought maybe you could return these. If you needed to."

"To buy the skateboards?" said Vicky, uncertainly.

"Yes . . . oh . . . oh . . . oh no!"

He was saying this because – perhaps

you've guessed – the tower of presents was beginning to topple.

Luckily his family sprang into action. His dad caught the *Millennium Falcon* and the helicopter and the walkie-talkie, his mum caught the crossbow and the tambourine, Ruby caught the pirate ship and digital alarm clock, the kite rose into the air anyway, Sam managed to hold on to the three juggling sticks, and the action figure of Spider-Man fell through the bars of Spock's cage and ended up upside down right next to the guinea pig. Who looked at it with quite a strong sense of, "Considering what you've just landed in, Spidey, I think you should change your catchphrase to, 'With great poo-wer, comes great res-poo-sibility.'"

Although that may be reading quite a lot into a guinea pig's face.

CHAPTER 25
THE ROZZERS

"**S**o . . . can you tell us some things about Samuel Bailey? Anyone?"

"I'm not speaking to the rozzers," whispered Grandpa Mike. "I've 'ad enough trouble in me life from them lot. Always lookin' over me shoulder, listenin' out for the *ner ner, ner ner, ner ner* on their cars. So don't expect me to 'elp 'em out now they need 'elp from me for once!"

The thing about this whisper, though, was that

it was one of those very loud whispers, where the person makes a very big thing of moving their mouth as well, so everyone there – Grandma Poppy, Grandma Glenda, Charlie, Vicky, Ruby, Sam, Carmel and DCI Bryant (and his assistant, PC Middleton) – obviously heard and understood what he said. Except for the children, who didn't understand that the word "rozzers" was slang for "police".

They were sitting in Carmel's office in Abbey Court. The police, who were looking for Grandpa Sam, had asked to speak to the whole family, and Abbey Court was the easiest place to do that. Carmel had had to bring in extra chairs to seat everyone.

'Sorry, sir," said DCI Bryant. "I do apologise if you feel you've been mistakenly placed on the wrong side of the law at any time."

Mike looked surprised at this, as if he couldn't understand how the policeman had heard his whisper, and then quite pleased at the idea that he was someone who had indeed spent time on the wrong side of the law.

"Yes, well, now you've admitted that, I s'pose I can tell you about Sam," he said. "He's a pain in the backside, to be honest."

"Don't say that about my husband! MY POOR LOST HUSBAND! AND TO A POLICEMAN AS WELL!!" screamed Grandma Poppy.

"Oh, sorry," said Mike.

"Hmm . . ." said DCI Bryant. "We might need a little bit more than that. He's been missing since . . . the night before last . . . ?"

"Nearly two whole days . . ." said Charlie. He looked very worried.

"'E's gone walkabout before!" said Grandpa Mike. "'E always comes back in the end . . ."

"Yes," said Carmel, "but he's never disappeared for as long as this."

"Have you searched all the usual places he's

gone before? In the local area?" said DCI Bryant.

"Yes," said Carmel. "I've been to the bus stop, the pub, the corner shop, the gym . . ."

"He goes to the gym?"

"Yes. X-sport, on the high street. Sometimes."

"And uses what machines?"

Everyone looked round. It was PC Middleton who had asked the question. He had his pen poised over a pad, waiting to jot down the answers. He had a strong accent, which later Vicky, who was from near there herself but who didn't sound quite as much like it, would explain to Sam and Ruby was a *Brummie* accent.

"Treadmill? Bench press? Pec deck? Leg curler?"

Carmel frowned, and looked confused. "No . . . he doesn't normally use the machines . . ."

"Oh," said PC Middleton. "Just classes, then? Pilates? Spinning? Yoga? Aerobics? Kickboxing?"

"No . . ." said Carmel. "He just . . . goes to the café.

Or stands around in the lobby . . . Last time, they called us because he was asking the receptionist for his pension."

"Asked the receptionist . . . for his . . . pension . . ." said PC Middleton, writing that down. While he did so, DCI Bryant was looking at him with quite a tired expression.

"Actually, I think recently he has tried to go in the pool . . ." said Carmel.

"Really? He swims?"

"Yes, he used to be really good at swimming, my dad . . ." said Vicky. "He was a local champion."

"Yes, but I'm afraid," said Carmel, "that he forgot, when he went in the pool at the gym, to bring any *trunks*."

There was a short, horrified pause as everyone took this in.

"Anything else that might be useful?" asked DCI Bryant. He looked around. No one seemed to be able to think of anything to say.

"He swears a lot . . ." said Sam, eventually.

"OK . . ." said DCI Bryant.

"Not bad swearwords. He makes them up. He called Grandpa Mike a boomdonking dipthong . . ."

"Yes. 'E did," said Grandpa Mike grimly. "I weren't too 'appy about it, neither . . ."

"And another time he called you a clodsmurfing jumbleweed. Actually," said Ruby.

Mike nodded even more grimly. His face was *very* grim by now, as he'd started this meeting looking fairly grim to make it clear to everyone that he wasn't too keen on meeting policemen. Not after his time inside. Even though, as we know, that didn't actually mean prison. What issues the police would have with him spending a lot of time in his house, I have no idea.

Everyone else, however – apart from Glenda, who was trying to share her husband's grimness – was smiling.

"Yes!" said Grandma Poppy. "And you, Glenda – he said you were a *grit-munching nerk*!! And that you should run a Grit-munching Nerk Station!"

That was it. Vicky, Charlie, Sam, Ruby, Carmel and even DCI Bryant burst out laughing.

"Boomdonking . . . dip . . . thong . . . how do you spell that?" asked PC Middleton, looking up from his pad.

"PC Middleton?" said DCI Bryant.

"Yes, sir?"

"Shut up."

"Right you are, sir."

"Well . . ." said DCI Bryant, getting up. "He sounds like quite a character, this Grandpa Sam."

"He is," said Vicky. "That's why we so want him back."

"I understand . . . OK. Well, we'll make some enquiries, and the local force will continue to keep an eye out for him. And . . ." he said, handing Charlie a card, "you can call me if you've got anything else you think of. Day or night."

Charlie nodded, and stood up. Then, everyone else got to their feet, apart from Grandma Glenda, who was still too miffed about everyone laughing at Grandpa Sam calling her a grit-munching nerk.

DCI Bryant shook hands with Vicky and Charlie. "Don't you worry, Mr and Mrs Green," he said, in what was clearly his deepest, most reassuring voice, "we'll find him."

"Thanks," said Vicky, sounding – and looking – tearful. "I hope so."

Suddenly, DCI Bryant turned to Sam. "Oh, and by the way, young man," he said, "happy birthday!"

Sam looked up at him. "How did you know that?"

"Aha!" he said. "I'm a detective. Here . . ." And he handed over a card. Sam looked at it: on the front was a photograph of a cat wearing an old-fashioned policeman's helmet. Inside, it said, *"To Sam! Happy birthday from everyone at Bracket Wood Police Station."* With loads of signatures underneath.

"That took quite a while, I might tell you, young man," said DCI Bryant. "Every single policeman and woman signed it . . . in the station."

"Well . . . thank you . . ." said Sam.

"Don't forget the present, sir!" said PC Middleton.

"Oh yes. And we made you this!"

He bent down. There was a cardboard box at his feet, which Sam hadn't noticed before. Out of it he produced a long wooden model of a building.

"Er . . . Thank you . . ." said Sam.

"It's a matchstick model of the station!" said DCI Bryant.

Sam (and his parents, and Ruby, and even Grandma Glenda, Grandma Poppy and Grandpa Mike) leant in for a closer look. It was actually very well done, with all the windows, and the steps up to the front door, and a sign saying HM Police: Bracket Wood Station. The words were made out of smaller matchsticks painted black.

"The DCI's a dab hand at matchstick models . . ." said PC Middleton.

"Well, yes, it is a hobby of mine. Although you were very helpful, Middleton. Collecting all the matchsticks, and lighting them, and then blowing them out. And everything."

"Right," said Sam, putting it down on the table. "Amazing. Thank you . . ."

"Actually meant that we didn't get the investigation into the whereabouts of Mr Bailey started on time, didn't it, sir?" said PC Middleton. "Held us back a whole day, making that . . ."

Sam stared at PC Middleton in horror. So that was why the police had been busy the day before? They'd been making him a *matchstick model*?

DCI Bryant stared at his colleague. "Middleton . . . ?"

"Have I said something wrong again, sir?"

"Yes."

"Right you are, sir." He did a zipping motion across his mouth. "I'll . . . y'know . . . zzzzzipppit! In future."

Then he looked at Sam. "Happy birthday, though."

Sam nodded, and said thank you politely, but really wanted to say two things.

1. It's not my birthday, and
2. This – everyone thinking it's my birthday – stops tonight.

CHAPTER 26
IT'S A DEAL

On the way home, Sam's parents stopped at the skate shop so they could buy him the skateboards – the last thing he needed for his secret project.

It made for an odd present-giving. A skateboard is quite hard to disguise in wrapping paper anyway, and the surprise element goes down with each one that emerges into the light. Particularly if the person getting the skateboard has already got the same skateboard – which is sitting on the floor next to him – and has written down a request for three more of the same.

And even more particularly if that child has waited outside the skate shop while you buy them.

But nonetheless, keen to show his parents he had changed, Sam stayed wide-eyed and positive, and made sure to say: "Oh! Thanks, Mum! Thanks, Dad!" after opening each one.

"That's OK, Sam," said Vicky.

"Yes," said Charlie. "Hope you enjoy them . . ."

"I will!" said Sam, picking up all four skateboards, one on top of the other. "Can I go and do my thing with these now?"

Charlie looked outside: it was a bright, sunny day, exactly the kind of day on which he would've loved to have gone out with *his* skateboard, thirty years ago.

"Yes, I don't see why not . . ."

Charlie said this, although a large part of him wanted to ask how exactly Sam was going to ride on four skateboards. Was he going to crouch on all fours? And then try to steer down the pavement a bit like an enormous beetle? That didn't sound very safe. He thought he'd better stay with him and check.

So he followed Sam out of the living room, and into the hallway. Charlie opened the front door for him, in fact. And then he stood there watching, as Sam walked past him, down the corridor, to his bedroom. Ten seconds later, the hammering started again.

Vicky appeared, looking down the hall, followed closely by Ruby, also looking down the hall. Charlie turned to his daughter.

"Ruby?" he said. "Can you find out what on earth he's *doing* in there?"

Ruby looked back at him. "Will you give me more pocket money?"

Vicky shook her head. "I don't think we can, love. We're really struggling to pay the bills because of Sam's birthdays . . ."

Charlie made a face, meaning, *yes, we are.* "But," he said, "the minute everything feels like we're *not* struggling so much any more, we'll buy you a—!"

"Kitten!" said Ruby.

"Well . . ." said Vicky.

"Um . . ." said Charlie.

"Great!" said Ruby. "Thanks, Mum! Thanks, Dad! It's a deal."

And she ran towards Sam's room. Charlie looked at Vicky.

"I was going to say new dress," he said.

Vicky nodded. "Too late now," she said.

CHAPTER 27
DON'T LOOK NOW

Ruby decided to wait until Sam was asleep. There were a number of reasons for this.

1. When she went to knock on his door, which she did straight after her dad had entrusted her with this mission, he didn't, like last time, get all grumpy with her and refuse to let her in for ages, but she did have to wait until he finished hammering. Then, when there was a moment's silence from inside and she knocked, her brother shouted,

"Hold on! Just a minute!" Followed by a lot of rustling. Ruby, being a very clever eight-year-old, knew this meant that he would be hiding whatever it was he was making. And, indeed, when Sam opened the door, the middle of the floor was covered by his duvet. Which, frankly, was a bit of a giveaway. But she pretended she hadn't noticed, and had just come in to feed Spock.

2. It felt more exciting and secret-agenty to creep in when he was asleep.

So that evening she let her mum and dad say goodnight, and kiss her gently on the forehead. She closed her eyes, and allowed them to think she'd gone to sleep really quickly. And then she whispered for nearly an hour to her monkeys (Ruby had a collection of furry, cuddly monkeys, all of whom had different names and different voices, who lived with her on her bed) in order to keep herself awake until she heard this conversation:

"Night, Mum! Night, Dad!"

"Shall we come and tuck you in?"

"No, no, Mum. I'm fine."

Which was, in fact, the conversation Sam had been having with his parents, just before he went to bed, for the last couple of nights. And then she listened for the sound of Sam doing something else he'd been doing for the last couple of nights, which was locking his bedroom door.

Except tonight there was no sound of that. Because when Ruby had gone into his room earlier in order to feed Spock, she'd hidden his key under some hay in the cage.

(I mentioned that Ruby was a very clever seven- (now eight)-year-old, right?)

Then she whispered to her monkeys for five

minutes longer, to be sure that Sam would be asleep. Then she crept out of her room, tiptoed carefully past the living room where her parents were watching TV, and gently opened the door to her brother's room.

So what she was *expecting* was to be able to easily see what Sam was building, because the duvet that was covering it would no longer be covering it: it would be on top of Sam. But it *was* still covering whatever the thing was Sam was building. It was also covering Sam. Because Sam was sleeping under his duvet, but also on top of the thing that was still in the middle of the floor.

Ruby knelt down. Her brother's face was calm and quiet. He was wearing his space pyjamas. She went over to where his feet were, and, very gently, lifted up the duvet.

Underneath was what appeared to be a platform – Sam had hammered together the six planks of wood,

securing them across with the coils of rope. In the coils of rope, on either side, he had put each of the two brooms. She looked further down, underneath the platform. Nailed to the underside were the skateboards: one beneath each corner.

Ruby frowned. This was very confusing. In her secret-agent persona, she wanted to report back to her boss – her dad – but at the moment she still didn't know what Sam was trying to make here. She heard a noise. It was Spock, scrabbling to the edge of the cage bars. She looked over at him. He looked over at her with quite a strong sense of, "Next time you want to *hide* something in my hay, I'd like a request in writing, if you don't mind!" And also, with quite a strong sense of – and this *wasn't* reading too much into a guinea pig's face, as the guinea pig in question was raising its face towards him, as if to make this clear – "Don't look now, but Sam's woken up."

CHAPTER 28
LIKE A SUPERHERO

"So . . ." said Sam, "what is it that is so interesting about my feet? That you can't wait until tomorrow morning to look at them?"

"Um . . ." said Ruby, touching his right foot, "well . . . this one is kind of ugly . . . but this one" – touching his left foot – "is almost pretty. As far as feet can be." She looked up. "Unusual for two feet from the same person to be so . . . different."

"OK."

"And, meanwhile, *what* are you lying on?"

"Oh. So *that's* what all this is about."

"Yes."

"Are you in the pay of Mum and Dad?"

"Well, if I can find out what you're up to, they've promised, at some point, to buy me a kitten!"

"So yes, basically."

"Yes."

"OK. I can't tell you."

"Why not?"

"Because they'll stop me from doing what . . . I need to do with it."

"What do you need to do with it?"

Sam sighed. He threw off the duvet, stood up then walked over to the window and looked out.

He put a finger to his lips, and, with his other hand, gestured for her to come over. She got up and walked towards him.

Sam pointed outside.

"Look . . ." he said.

Ruby stood on tiptoe. "I can't really see out of the window," she said.

Sam looked at her. He nodded. He went over to the other side of his bed-platform, knelt down and pushed. On its four skateboards, it wheeled over to the window.

"Stand on that . . ." he said. So she did. It gave her just the right amount of height to see clearly out of the window. From here, the seventeenth floor, the lights of the city were glittering all around.

"Now look . . ." he said, pointing again.

She followed the direction of his finger, scrunching up her eyes.

"What am I looking for?"

"On the river. That island . . ."

She scrunched up her eyes even more. "I still can't see . . ."

"Hold on," said Sam. "Try this."

She unscrunched her eyes. Standing behind her, Sam was now holding something in front of her face.

"What is it?" asked Ruby, pulling back.

"It's my new invention," said Sam with a hint of pride. "The *binocuscope*."

Ruby looked at what he was holding in front of her eyes. It was Sam's binoculars. These, you may remember, had got broken. But the lenses and the bit you look through were still fine. Sam had attached these to the second half of the telescope tube, the part with the strong lens on the end. It looked like this.

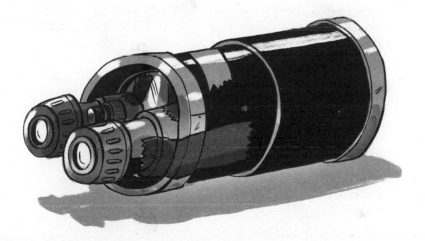

"Oh right," said Ruby. "That's clever." And she put her eyes against the binocuscope.

It *was* clever. Because suddenly she could see. All the way down towards the river, and the little island in the middle of it. She could see the water around it, the reflection of the lights on the surface and the trees that seemed to cover every millimetre of the bank. That seemed to be all. But then, in the middle of the trees, she saw it. A light. It flashed, or rather glowed, brightly, once, and then vanished.

There was something beautiful about it, thought Ruby. Something magical.

"What is it?"

"A star," said Sam.

Ruby took her eyes off the binocuscope, and looked at her brother doubtfully.

"A star? Why isn't it in the sky?" she said.

"It fell out."

"Fell out? I'm really not sure that happens."

"I saw it! And they do vanish from the sky sometimes!"

"Yes. It's called a supernova, actually. They explode. They don't *fall out.*"

"I saw it, Ruby! I know you know lots about stars and astrology—"

"Astronomy."

"That too . . . but I promise you, I saw it!"

Ruby looked out at the sky. She nodded. One of the things she had learnt through reading a lot about stars and astrology – sorry, astronomy – is that there are many things about the universe that remain unknowable.

"OK. I believe you, Sam. When did you see it?"

"The night of my . . . birthday. You know. When I wished my birthday could be every day. Which" – and now Sam looked out of the window – "is what I don't want any more . . ."

"You don't?" said Ruby.

"No."

"Why?"

"Because I just want to look for Grandpa Sam! And Mum and Dad are spending so much time and money on my birthday that it's getting in the way of finding him . . ." He paused. "It's getting in the way – so I'm going to make it stop."

He looked at his sister very intensely, and said, also very intensely, like he was a superhero who had finally worked out how to save the world: *"I'm going to un-wish my wish."*

CHAPTER 29
SKATEBOAT

Ruby frowned. "Maybe your wish was nothing to do with the star, though."

Which brought Sam down to earth a bit. Now it was his turn to frown. "What do you mean?"

"Well, maybe it just fell out of the sky because . . . I dunno . . . it bumped into another star. Or an asteroid. Or maybe Zeus *pulled* it out."

"Zeus doesn't exist. I'd have thought you'd be the first to point that out."

"Well, neither do stars that live on islands. Actually."

"Look," said Sam, "all I know is that I saw a star. I wished my birthday was every day. The star fell out of the sky. And then everyone started behaving as if it *was* my birthday every day. Even you."

Ruby nodded. "I did," she said. "Actually."

Sam looked out of the window. "And now there's a light shining on that island. Which was right underneath where the star fell out of the sky. So I've got a plan to go there – to get to that island – and wish on that star again, to make my birthday *not* be every day."

"Right . . ." said Ruby. "I see. And so your plan is?"

Sam continued to look out of the window. Then he turned and looked at her.

"That thing you're standing on. That I was sleeping on. That I've built. With stuff from my birthday list?"

"Yes?"

"It's a boat. Or it will be."

Ruby looked down at the platform. She got off it. She examined it.

"What are the skateboards for?"

Sam looked at her as if that was obvious. "So that I can slide it down to the river. It's a skateboard-cum-boat. A skateboat!"

And even though Ruby was a very clever eight-year-old who knew about stars and astrology – arrggh! astronomy – there was a part of her that was still just an eight-year-old. And eight-year-olds sometimes just accept what they're told in a very straightforward way.

Which is why she nodded, and then looked up at him and said:

"Can I come?"

PART 4

AND SO SAY
ALL OF US

CHAPTER 30
OVER THE WAVES
OF A CONCRETE SEA

"Shh!" said Sam.

"I'm being as quiet as I can . . ." whispered Ruby. "Considering what we're doing here is carrying a skateboat out of your room . . ."

"Shh!"

"OK, right. Shh it is."

It's not easy, this, though, was what she wanted to say. She was a lot smaller than Sam, even though he had by now started to get back down to his normal size, and so between them they were holding the skateboat at quite a sharp downwards angle. It wasn't as heavy as she thought it was going to be, but it was awkward. Not least because when she turned her head to the right or left, her ears would hit a skateboard wheel. It wasn't made any easier by the fact that Sam had said they had to bring the binocuscope as well, which kept on rolling backwards and forwards on the wooden boards.

"Shhhhh!!" said Sam again, a bit unnecessarily, as Ruby hadn't said anything. But they were in the hallway, passing the door to the living room, where their parents were watching TV. The time was 10pm.

Sam and Ruby had on two sets of clothes: because it was September, and starting to get cold, and they were going out in the middle of the night.

As they went through the front door, Ruby whispered: "Should we leave them a note?"

"Who?"

"Mum and Dad, of course!"

"Oh!" said Sam. "No, it'll be fine. They'll never even notice we've gone."

They got the skateboat out of the door of their flat easily enough. Not so easily into the lift: Sam had to press his body face-forward against the wall and Ruby had to crouch underneath the skateboat, which was lying diagonally over her head.

"This is horrible, Sam!" she shouted. "I'm too close to the toilet smell! Wee! My nose is near the wee smell!"

"OK, OK!" he said. "Sorry!" Sam reached round for the buttons, and, after some fumbling, pressed G, for Ground Floor.

Down they went, Ruby holding her nose, and indeed breath, all the way.

The lift opened, and they crashed the skateboat through the doors of Noam Chomsky House on to the path, which curved through some sparsely

planted trees, down the hill and out to the road.

Then Sam put his left foot on the skateboat, pushed with his right to get going and immediately fell over. The skateboat went off the path into the grass verge.

"Ow!" he said. "Sorry. Don't know why that happened. Let's get it and try again."

And they did. And he fell off again.

"Ow!"

Ruby watched, deadpan. "Have you, by any chance, tried riding this before? At all?"

"No," said Sam, getting up, "but I thought it would be just like riding a skateboard. Only bigger."

"Yes, I think that 'only bigger' thing may make quite a *big* difference . . ."

"Hmm . . . don't quite know what to do . . ." said Sam.

"Hello!" said a voice. They both looked round.

"Oh, right . . ." said Sam. "Hi, Zada. This is my sister, Ruby."

"Hello!" said Zada.

"Hello . . ." said Ruby suspiciously. For no real reason. She was just like that with new people.

"So . . ." said Zada, looking at the skateboat, "what happened to your board? Did it have . . . an allergic reaction to something . . . ?"

"Eh?" said Sam. "Oh! No!"

"It's a long story," said Ruby, still suspicious, and not really wanting to explain to Zada what they were trying to do.

"OK!" she replied, shrugging. "But I saw you fall off it. Do you want some help?"

Sam looked at the skateboat. Then back at her.

"You think you could help me ride this board too?"

Zada looked at it. "Yes." She got on the skateboat. "It's bigger, isn't it? Than a normal board. So. It's just a question of . . ." And she put her foot down firmly on the floor, "doing everything – all your movements, all your weight-shifting – *bigger* . . ."

The skateboat moved off towards the bowl under Noam Chomsky House. Sam and Ruby glanced at each other. Zada wasn't going to . . . was she . . . ?

But she did. She stuck out her arms in a flying shape, and then leant towards the left. The skateboat moved, slowly, at first, and then disappeared down below Noam Chomsky House.

Ruby and Sam ran over to see Zada on the skateboat, gliding, not effortlessly, but getting more fluid by the second, around the bowl. Up the ramp, down the ramp, around the sides – all the time holding out her arms, like an old-fashioned child pretending to be an aeroplane. As she got better and better, she actually made it seem like she was on a boat, sailing over the waves of a concrete sea.

"This is what you need to do!" she shouted as she

went. "Just place your weight more firmly – and use your arms more!"

Then Zada pushed off again round a curve, and up towards where her little audience were watching. As a last flourish, just before she got to them, she added an Olly 360, no pivot, lifting herself in the air and twisting round like a ballet dancer to arrive the right way round by the time the board stopped at an awestruck Sam and Ruby.

"So. That is it, really. All yours!" she said.

CHAPTER 31
BRICK. WALL.

From the top of the path, Sam held the skateboat steady with his foot. Zada had vanished almost as quickly as she'd appeared. Ruby looked at Sam doubtfully.

"Do you think that was enough? Zada's lesson?"

Sam didn't answer that question. He held the binocuscope up to his eyes, and looked down towards the river. Ruby got up on to the skateboat, and stood on tiptoe, trying to see with her eyes.

"Can you see it?" she said. "The star?"

"Yes . . ." said Sam, still looking through the lens. "It seems to be getting fainter, though . . ."

"Fainter?"

"Yes. Maybe it's dying." He put down the binocuscope. "Not in a supernova, explosive way. Just in a kind of not-where-it's-meant-to-be kind of way. Like a fish out of water."

This interested Ruby, and she strained even further on her tiptoes, trying to see the star. Then she noticed that someone was placing something on her head. It was Sam, and the thing was a helmet, his spare skateboard helmet. She looked up. His was already on. He smiled at her.

"So we'd better get going!" he said. And, with that, he planted one foot firmly on top of the skateboat, kicked his other foot – the one on the ground – backwards and down the hill they went.

"WHAAAAAA!!!!" went Ruby. They were going very, very fast.

"Hold on!" shouted Sam.

"I AM HOLDING ON! TO YOUR LEG! I STILL HAVE TO SCREAM!!"

"But it's fun! Isn't it?"

"IT IS FUN! BUT FRIGHTENING AS WELL!!! WHAAAAAAAA!! BUT ALSO . . . YEEEEHAAAAAA!!"

This was the point when they came off the path up to Noam Chomsky House, and on to the street, Geary Road. And headed straight towards a brick wall.

"Uh-oh . . ." said Sam.

"BRICK WALL, SAM!" shouted Ruby. "BRICK. WALL."

"I KNOW!"

"REMEMBER WHAT ZADA SAID!"

"YES! OK!"

He pressed his foot down to the right to turn, like he would on his normal board. But the skateboat didn't move. It carried on heading straight at the wall!

"IT'S NOT MOVING!" shouted Sam.

"MORE WEIGHT!" shouted Ruby. "REMEMBER HOW SHE DID IT!"

Sam pressed his foot down harder. Still nothing. The wall was centimetres away. He pressed harder again. He raised his arms in the flying pose Zada had done, and leant down, his arms going diagonal, to the right. And closed his eyes. Which Zada hadn't done. But then Zada didn't seem to feel fear.

Sam was aware of something moving behind him, but it was too late to look round. He braced himself for the crash . . .

. . . and then, at the last minute, the skateboat swerved away and trundled on down the pavement.

"Phew!" he said. "That was lucky!"

"Well," said Ruby. "Lucky-ish . . ."

Sam looked round. Ruby had moved to the far right edge of the skateboat. And was also doing the flying-arms-diagonal thing. It was *her* weight that had made the difference.

"Oh . . ." he said, "that's clever."

"Yes," said Ruby. "And don't worry – I'll shift along

behind you every time we need to turn from now on . . ."

Sam smiled at her, nodding.

"What a great sister you are, Ruby!" he said.

Ruby smiled. "I am," she said. "Actually."

CHAPTER 32
A FEELING

"Charlie . . ." said Vicky, turning the TV down on the remote control.

"Hmmm . . . ?" said Charlie.

"Do you mind checking on the kids?"

Charlie glanced over to his phone, lying on the coffee table.

"It's past ten o' clock . . ." he said. "They'll be fast asleep."

"Yes," said Vicky.

"So . . . they're not babies. Why do you want me to check on them?"

"I don't know. Just a feeling . . ."

Charlie looked at his wife. "Really, love . . . you know I've always been happy to go along with your feelings. *But*, in general, I think there's more important things to do with our time than whatever our feelings tell us to do. I think it might be time to grow up and base our life on facts and reason and not whatever you mean by 'a feeling'."

"Fine," said Vicky, getting up. "If you don't want to miss a second of *Match of the Day*, I'll do it."

"No, no!" said Charlie crossly. "Don't worry. I'll go." And he leapt up, with a stride that said OK-then-I'm-going-to-prove-a-point-to-you-even-though-I-really-want-to-keep-watching-TV and walked out of the living room.

Four minutes later, he came back again. And said:

"Um . . . darling?"

"Yes?"

"I think your feeling may have been . . . right."

CHAPTER 33
THE ONE THING YOU DEFINITELY NEED ON A DANGEROUS SECRET MISSION

The skateboat slowed down as the streets became less steep.

Sam stuck to the pavement. He knew he wasn't supposed to skateboard there, but it was obviously safer than the road, and at this time of the night there were hardly any pedestrians. In fact, it was almost *too* safe, because now they were virtually not moving at all.

"OK . . ." he said to Ruby, "get your broom out."

"Pardon?"

"You remember – well, you can see – there's a broom held inside the ropes? Two of them, one on either side?"

"Yes . . . ?"

Sam lifted the broom nearest him out of its rope harness, and pointed to the other one. "Get that one out. We need some elbow grease to get us through this bit."

"Elbow . . . ?"

"Hold it at the top. And push . . . like this."

He demonstrated, leaning over and pushing away from the ground with the brush of the broom. The skateboat moved, although not in a straight line.

"You have to do it at the same time. Otherwise we'll go round in a circle!"

Ruby took out the broom on her side.

"All right . . ." she said. "Although I don't remember where I signed up for street cleaning!"

But when she followed his lead, and pushed against the pavement with her broom at the same time, it worked! The skateboat picked up speed again!

Although this time it felt more under control. So Ruby didn't feel the need to scream so loudly or so often. Everything went quiet. All that could be heard was the *clop clop clop* of the wheels as they moved over the paving stones, the *woosh woosh woosh* of the wind around them, the *brush brush brush* of the brooms on the ground and the *squeak squeak squeak* of the . . .

The *squeak squeak squeak* of the . . .

What *was* that squeaking noise?

"Is that the wheels?" said Ruby.

"Maybe . . ." said Sam, crouching down to look closely at the area the noise was coming from.

Squeak. Squeak.

"Perhaps the skateboard wheels need oiling – or the trucks . . ." he said. "Hold on . . ." he added. "If we start heading towards a wall again, let me know."

"Actually," said Ruby. "I will."

Sam bent down further and, with the ground rushing by his nose, looked underneath the vehicle.

There was a short pause. His face went very deadpan. Then he reached underneath as if to adjust something . . . and said:

"Or . . . perhaps someone decided to come with us."

He pulled out from under the skateboat a small, furry creature. Who, in the light shining down from one of the streetlamps, was looking at Ruby with quite a strong sense of, "If you're going on a dangerous secret mission, the one thing you *definitely* need with you is a guinea pig."

CHAPTER 34
ALTOGETHER A STRANGE SIGHT

Sam stopped the skateboat by putting his foot down hard on the ground. He stared at Spock for a while, before handing him to Ruby.

"How did *he* get under there?" she asked.

"I don't know . . ." said Sam. "Maybe we knocked the cage open as we were carrying the skateboat out . . . ?"

Spock looked at them with quite a strong sense of, "Yes, you did. It was very traumatic and I had to run away from the noise, and the only place I could find to hide was between the top bit of wood and the bit of wood with wheels on it." He had a very expressive face, that guinea pig.

"What shall we do?" said Ruby. "We can't turn back now!"

"No, we can't. Apart from anything, it's downhill all the way to the river. Which means it's uphill all the way back home."

Ruby paused from thinking about Spock for a second. "So . . . how *were* you planning to get us home?"

Sam frowned. "Oh. I hadn't really thought that far."

Squeak squeak squeak, went Spock.

"OK. Let's not worry about it for the moment. He'll just have to come with us."

"OK," said Ruby.

Sam nodded and kicked off. The skateboat moved. Because they'd stopped and because it was no longer downhill, he really had to put his back into it. Four kicks down the line, they'd finally built up speed, which left him breathless. That was when he looked round, and saw that Ruby had put Spock on top of her helmet.

The guinea pig was looking out into the night with quite a strong sense of, "This is fun. I think I look like one of those statues of half-naked ladies they used to have on the front of old boats."

"*What are you doing?*" said Sam to Ruby.

"When we turn, I have to move about and grab on to the boards with both hands to shift my weight across. So where else am I going to put him?"

Sam shook his head. But then suddenly he didn't have time to think about it any more, as he heard the sound of a siren.

He looked around. Coming out of the corner, at great speed – a corner they were approaching – was a police car. *Wah-wah! Wah-wah! Wah-wah!* was what Sam felt inside – but it was also the sound of the siren. Sam put his arms back up into the flying position, and shouted, "Left!"

Ruby moved – still fast, but, because she had a guinea pig on her head, a little more carefully than usual – to the left. If you were walking down the street, and watching very closely, you may have noticed that the guinea pig on her head, at the same time, also leant to the left.

And the skateboat turned left into a new street, and there it was: the river.

CHAPTER 35
KEEP IT ZIPPED

"Calm down, Mrs Green," said DCI Bryant. "We will *find* your children!"

"Yes," said PC Middleton. "Even though we've completely failed, up to this point, to find your father . . ."

This made Vicky, who'd been crying hysterically for some time, cry even more. It also made DCI Bryant stare at PC Middleton for some time.

PC Middleton nodded to himself. "Have I said something stupid again, sir?" he said.

DCI Bryant nodded in turn, gesturing with his head towards Vicky, who now had her face in her hands.

"Thought so. *Zzzzzzzip!*" said PC Middleton, doing the motion across his mouth again.

"I don't know what's happening to us!" sobbed Vicky. "Our family is falling apart! And we've been trying so hard, making sure Sam has a really nice birthday, every day!"

"Yes, darling," said Charlie, who was sitting behind her, rubbing her back. DCI Bryant sipped his tea, discreetly, waiting for her to calm down. PC Middleton looked on, jotting things down in his notebook.

"Any unusual activity or suchlike?" said DCI Bryant eventually. "From your son?"

"Well . . . there is something," said Charlie. "There's been a lot of banging and nailing and general kind of . . . building sounds coming from Sam's room over the last few days . . ."

"Right . . . have you got that, Middleton?"

"Writing it down, sir."

"We actually asked Ruby to see if she could find out what it was. Because Sam wouldn't let us into his room . . ."

"Hold on . . ." said PC Middleton, scribbling. "Wouldn't . . . let . . . us . . . into his room . . ."

"Don't write 'us', Middleton."

PC Middleton frowned. "But that's what Mr Green said."

"Yes, but if you write 'us', when you look back at your notes, it will look like Sam hadn't let *you and me* into his room. Won't it?"

PC Middleton looked down at his pad, confused.

"And, knowing you, you'll find that confusing, won't you?" DCI Bryant continued.

PC Middleton considered this for a moment. "Yes. You're right, sir. I will. Absolutely." He looked down again, frowning even harder. Then looked up. "So . . . what shall I write?"

"*Mr and Mrs Green*. Sam wouldn't let *Mr and Mrs Green* into his room!"

"Oh! Yes!" He crossed out what he'd written before, and started again.

"Any other information, Mr Green? Mrs Green?" said DCI Bryant.

"Well," said Vicky, "there's his birthday lists. Over the last few days . . ."

"Yes . . ." said Charlie, unfolding one, and handing it over. DCI Bryant scanned it with his eyes. Then, read out loud:

"1. Six large planks of wood.

2. A hammer and some nails.

3. Six coils of rope.

4. A roll of gaffer tape.

5. Two brooms."

He looked up. "So he was making something. It sounds like . . . a door? Maybe?"

"Or a box?" said Charlie.

"A sofa?" said PC Middleton.

DCI Bryant stared at him. "Well, clearly it's not a sofa, Middleton. There are no cushions on the list. Or any springs."

"Stupid idea, sir?"

"Yes, Middleton."

"Right you are." He did the zipping motion again. "And this time I'll keep it . . ." He did the zipping motion AGAIN. With quite a loud *zzzzippp!* sound.

DCI Bryant turned back to Charlie and Vicky.

"Anything else you can think of? What does Sam like? Hobbies et cetera . . . ?"

The Greens looked at each other. Their faces, already worried, betrayed a small element of sadness.

"Well . . ." said Vicky, blinking away the tears, "he used to like lots of things. Sci-fi. Building models of rocket ships and cars and stuff. But recently he's become a bit . . ." She looked across at her husband. He nodded, understanding.

"Truth is, we don't quite know what he likes any more. He seems not to like anything that much . . ." Charlie's voice went down, almost to a whisper. "He's become . . . a bit of a different boy . . ."

"Skateboards!" said Vicky suddenly.

"Sorry?" said DCI Bryant.

"He used to like skateboards. And that hasn't changed! Because recently he asked for another one. More than one, in fact!"

"Yes," said Charlie, "he did! We got him one, and then recently he asked for three more."

"He's got four skateboards?" said DCI Bryant.

"Yes."

"And where are they now?"

Vicky and Charlie looked at each other.

"I don't know. I couldn't see them in his room when we searched up there," said Vicky.

"Right . . . so it's possible that your son and your daughter have gone somewhere on the skateboards?"

"Well . . ." said Charlie. "I don't know. Ruby doesn't really skate . . . and why would they take all four?"

"I don't know," said DCI Bryant, his face going into a face not unlike the ones he had seen on the TV in crime shows, where the detective is doing some hard thinking. "If you put six planks of wood together with four skateboards . . . what would that look like? What would that make?"

"MMMMMMM!! MMMMMM!!"

Charlie, Vicky and DCI Bryant looked round. It was PC Middleton.

"MMMMMM! MMMMMM!" he continued.

"Middleton . . ." said DCI Bryant. "Are you all right? Are you having some sort of fit?"

With his right index finger, PC Middleton pointed to his mouth.

"You've bitten your tongue?"

PC Middleton shook his head. He waved his left hand in front of his mouth.

"You've burnt your hand?"

"MMMMM! MMMMM!"

"I think, DCI Bryant . . ." said Vicky gently, "that PC Middleton is asking if he can . . . er . . . unzip his mouth."

PC Middleton did a big thumbs-up at Vicky, pointing at her at the same time with his other hand.

DCI Bryant stared at PC Middleton for some small time. Then he said: "*Really?* That's really what you're trying to say?"

PC Middleton nodded his head. DCI Bryant

nodded as well, while sighing very, very deeply.

"OK, Middleton. You can unzip your mouth."

PC Middleton did so, with a very big, "ZZZIIIPPPP!"

"Oh, that's better," he said, breathing out heavily.

"So . . . !" said DCI Bryant. "What is it? What did you want to say?"

"Oh! Yes! Well! You know when we were driving here?"

"Yes . . ."

"And you were fiddling with the radio?"

"Well. Yes." DCI Bryant glanced at Charlie and Vicky. "To keep contact with the station, of course . . ."

"No, you were trying to get *The Organist Entertains* on Radio Two. You always like to listen to that."

DCI Bryant frowned, and raised his hand as if to tell PC Middleton to zip it again. But then thought better of it.

"Anyway," continued PC Middleton, "while you

were doing that, we nearly hit two children."

Charlie and Vicky and DCI Bryant were open-mouthed.

"WHAT?" said DCI Bryant.

"Yes. They were coming down the road the other way on a . . . well. If I had to describe it, I'd say it was . . . six planks of wood mounted on four skateboards."

Charlie and Vicky and DCI Bryant's mouth stayed open.

DCI Bryant said:

"And . . . and . . . you didn't think to mention it? At all?"

"Well. They swerved past us fine. No bother. And you know. I didn't want to disturb you during *The Organist Entertains*."

There was a long pause, during which Charlie and Vicky and DCI Bryant all continued to stare at PC Middleton.

"You know what?" he said, eventually. "I think next time I'll just keep it zipped."

CHAPTER 36
HOW MUCH OF AN IDIOT IS HE?

"So when you told me about this plan," Ruby was saying, "you said this was . . . a boat."

Sam nodded. He was looking out at the river. Slowly, he raised the binocuscope to his eyes. Through the double lens, merging into one as his vision grew used to it, he could see the island, covered in trees. It was exactly halfway across the river, between the north and south of the city.

He swung the 'scope this way and that, seeing the

foliage pass by his eyes: but could find no sign of a light. Surely a star, a fallen star . . . its light couldn't just go out?

"Sam!" said Ruby again. She was standing by the skateboat. It had come to rest by some railings overlooking the river.

"Yes," he said, putting the binocuscope down, but continuing to look out. The river was calm – perhaps it always was, not being the sea, and therefore not really having waves – but it looked very deep.

"Have you tested the . . . boatworthiness of this skateboat? In any way?" she asked.

"Boatworthiness?" Sam said, still looking out. "Is that even a word?"

"Riverworthiness. Staying-on-top-of-waterworthiness." She reached up and pulled his face round towards hers. "How do we know it's going to *float*?"

Sam looked at her (he didn't really have any choice). "Oh yes, I've done all sorts of exact calculations.

Weight, surface area, marine biology, et cetera, et cetera."

"Have you?"

"No."

"Oh."

Sam looked at the skateboat, and said, "Well, it got us here OK! Didn't it? All the way from where we live."

"Yes . . ." said Ruby.

"And it's *much* less far to over there. Where the island is."

Ruby turned to the skateboat, on which Spock was sitting, looking up at her with quite a strong sense of, "How much of an idiot *is* he?"

"Come on," said Sam, going round to the other side of the skateboat.

Ruby came round and stood next to him. "Come on what?"

"Come on, let's get the skateboat down the bank."

"How are we going to do that?"

Sam looked at her as if it was obvious. "Ollie," he said.

And then he leapt, as high as he could, and landed with his entire weight on the back of the boards. The head of the skateboat flipped up, enough, as he planned, to force the front wheels over the railings.

Unfortunately, as he *hadn't* planned, the force was also enough to flip Spock into the air.

Sam and Ruby looked up to see the guinea pig flying high in the night sky, looking down on them with quite a strong sense of, "Oh, I see: *this* much of an idiot."

CHAPTER 37
SCHROPPLINGYTHINGY

Confirming, to some extent, Spock's opinion of him, Sam just continued to watch, idiotically, as he – Spock – started to dip down.

The guinea pig must have reached about six metres up, which was both impressive, if you are into watching small rodents take flight, and useful, because it gave Ruby, who chose not to just watch idiotically, time to squeeze through the railings and roll down the bank towards the edge of the river.

"Ruby!" shouted Sam, shaken out of his Spock-watching trance for fear of his little sister's safety. "Don't go too near the water!"

Ruby stood up. She was, in fact, standing right by the water. In quite a lot of mud.

"I'm just trying to catch— Oh!" she said.

She'd been about to say – and this may be obvious – "Spock". She'd been leaning over the river, trying to catch Spock.

Unfortunately, Spock landed in the river away from her outstretched arms, with quite a strong sense of . . . *PLOP!*

"Spock! Spock!"

Now I know what you're thinking. You're thinking: *Oh my goodness, can guinea pigs swim?*

Turns out, yes they can. But they don't look very comfortable doing it. A lot less comfortable than fish. And even less comfortable than cats.

Spock, particularly, did not look comfortable in the river, in the middle of the night. His little face poked above the water, with, this time, a look that didn't say anything strongly. Just . . . panic.

"Sam! Sam!" shouted Ruby. "What are we going to do?" She moved towards the water, as if about to dive in.

"Don't!" shouted Sam from above. "OK! Let's go!" He pushed the skateboat from behind, over the railings. It bumped and cracked as it went over, but got there, sliding down the grassy bank and coming to a halt in the mud right by Ruby.

Sam jumped over the railings and ran down the bank. He pushed the skateboat further into the river.

"Is it going to float, Sam? Is it?" said Ruby.

"Just believe, Ruby. Believe in the skateboat. Believe in the skateboat." He put his hands on her shoulders. "And it *will* float."

Ruby looked at him. "Really?" she said, raising an eyebrow.

"I dunno," said Sam, taking his hands off her

shoulders. "That's the sort of thing people say in films."

They both looked out to where Spock was treading water. The skateboat was at that point not visible. It seemed to have mainly submerged. It may, in fact, not have deserved the name *boat*, and would have been better described as just some-sinking-planks-of wood.

"I don't think the believing is working," said Ruby.

"But we haven't got anything else at this stage, I'm afraid," said Sam.

"Yes," said Ruby. "I get that. Shall we name it something?"

"What?"

"The skateboat." She looked over at the dark water. "It might help."

Sam shrugged. "What were you thinking?"

Ruby thought for a second, and then said: "Schrodinger."

"Bless you," said Sam.

"No. That's what I want to call the skateboat. Schrodinger."

Sam frowned. "Why?"

"He was a scientist. He wrote about physics. He did an experiment about a cat. About how sometimes a cat can be there and not there."

"Right. Not sure we've really got time for this, Ruby, and poor Spock is—"

"I don't really understand it, to be honest. But I know the skateboat is there, under the water, even though we can't see it. So it's as if the skateboat – like that cat – is sort of there and not there. So: Schrodinger."

Sam took a deep breath. His sister was sometimes very confusing. But it wasn't worth arguing.

"OK, that's its name, Schropplingythingy—"

"Schrodinger . . ."

"Whatever."

And, with that, they both shut their eyes, and

believed: they both focused and concentrated. Sam and Ruby imagined *Schrodinger* the skateboat floating above the water, sailing easily like it was Noah's ark.

And when they opened their eyes it *was* above the water. *Schrodinger* had come back up again!

"It worked, Sam! It worked!" said Ruby.

"Yes. To be honest, I prefer to think that's because I designed *Schrobangbang* very cleverly to be seaworthy—"

"Who cares! Let's get on! We need to rescue Spock."

CHAPTER 38
BON VOYAGE

Ruby was already wading into the river. Sam went after her, and, making sure she didn't get too wet, grabbed her by the underarms and lifted her on to the skateboat. In doing so, he, himself, however, got completely soaked. The river was very cold, much colder than he expected. Quickly, he got on the skateboat too, which wasn't easy. Every time he put his arms on to push himself on to it, the other side went right up in the air (and the part he was pushing went down into the water). Eventually, he managed it by getting on sideways, and rolling his body on to the planks.

"Are you OK?" said Ruby.

"Yes . . ." he said, although his teeth were chattering. "Now! Get your broom!"

"My broom?"

"Yes!" he said, picking his up.

"But . . . there's no pavement to push against?"

"It's now an oar!"

Sam dunked his broom into the river. Ruby, understanding, gave him a thumbs-up, and held hers towards the water too.

"OK! Now when I say row . . . row!!"

"OK . . . hold on a minute!"

"What?"

"Where's Spock gone?"

They both looked out. Nothing. Blackness.

"Where *is* he?" repeated Ruby frantically.

Then, above the quiet lapping of the water against the skateboat, they heard a noise. *Scrunch. Chew chew chew. Scrunch.*

It was coming from behind them. They looked round to see, on the bank, Spock, tucking into a manky, muddy apple core.

As the skateboat moved away from the shore, Spock looked up briefly from his chewing, with quite a strong sense on his tiny face of, *"Bon voyage."*

CHAPTER 39
LET'S GO

"So, Middleton," said DCI Bryant, shutting the door of his police car. "Where exactly did you see the children on top of their . . ."

"I'd call it a skateboat, sir."

"A skateboat . . . ?" said DCI Bryant, frowning, tasting the phrase. He turned the key. The engine flared, then hummed. "OK. Anyway. Where?"

"As we were passing Bracket Wood School. We turned up the road, into it, and that was definitely when . . ."

"The skateboat came down the street?"

"No, that's when you put on *The Organist Entertains*."

DCI Bryant stared at him. He took a deep breath. He turned round.

"All belted up?"

Charlie and Vicky, sitting in the back, looking pale and frightened, nodded.

"OK. Let's go," said DCI Bryant, pressing his foot to the accelerator.

CHAPTER 40
EXTREMELY DARK AND MUDDY

It wasn't, it turned out, all that easy to row a skateboat using brooms. The brooms had been quite successful as pushers when *Schrodinger* had been on the road, but now that they were pushing against water there was a problem, which was that the brushes became very wet. Which made them very heavy to lift out of the water. Which made rowing *Schrodinger* – which, frankly, was feeling less like a boat and more like a very rudimentary raft – very, very difficult.

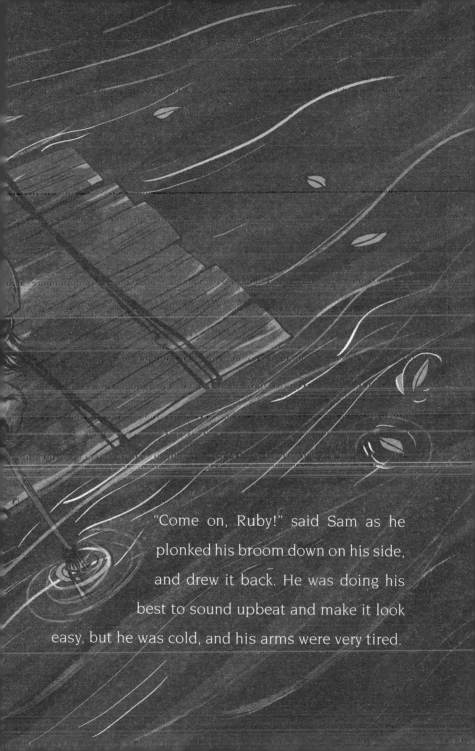

"Come on, Ruby!" said Sam as he
plonked his broom down on his side,
and drew it back. He was doing his
best to sound upbeat and make it look
easy, but he was cold, and his arms were very tired.

"I'm cold! And my arms are very tired!" shouted Ruby, sounding as if she was speaking from inside his head.

"I know!" Sam shouted back. "Same with me! But we're not far away now!"

"That's what Mum and Dad say when we're driving somewhere on holiday! And it's not true then, either!"

"No, it *is* true this time! The island's only about fifty metres away!" Which *was* true. But fifty metres in a car would've truly been not far away. Fifty metres in a skateboat rowed with sodden brooms across a river in the middle of the night felt like a million miles. At least it did to a very tired and cold eight-year-old girl and eleven-year-old boy.

Sam gazed across towards the island. It looked extremely dark and muddy and full of not very friendly trees. It *didn't* look, to be honest, like somewhere that was worth taking a lot of effort to get to. It looked more like somewhere worth taking a lot of effort to run away from.

It struck him that this whole thing may have been a terrible mistake. It was, for a start, dangerous. He was a kid. His sister, however smart she was, was an even younger kid. And they may have had brooms and ropes and four skateboards presently under the water, but one thing they didn't have, he suddenly noticed for the first time, was lifejackets.

In desperation, he raised the binocuscope to his eyes. This wasn't easy, as he was still rowing with his broom hand, and keeping the device still in front of his face wasn't easy either. It wobbled, and trembled, and it was really hard to see *anything*.

Please, Sam thought, *please. At least make this danger worthwhile. Please, star. Shine.*

CHAPTER 41
MIDNIGHT FEAST

"**O**K, Mr and Mrs Green. We have all our units in the local area out looking for your children. The main thing, for now, is that you stay calm and – OH MY G—!"

This was DCI Bryant, who had been driving around the Bracket Wood School area for twenty minutes. On seeing no immediate sight of the children, he had turned round, and begun to head back towards Noam Chomsky House – he was, in fact, just passing

Abbey Court – when three people in dressing gowns holding plastic bags suddenly stepped out into the middle of the road.

DCI Bryant slammed on the brakes. PC Middleton, Charlie and Vicky were all thrown forward in their seat belts, but the car slid screeching to a halt just in time. Just in time, that is, to avoid hitting Grandpa Mike, Grandma Glenda and Grandma Poppy.

Who didn't seem to be too bothered about the fact that they had almost been run down. They just stood there, looking at the car.

DCI Bryant pressed a button; the window came down.

"Excuse me? What are you doing?"

"Oh, hello, Officer!" said Poppy.

"You're a lovely young man!" said Glenda.

"Oh no, it's the rozzers!" said Mike.

"Stop speaking like that, Michael!" said Poppy.

"Eh?"

"All the silly stuff you say about the police! And being inside! Like you're a hardened criminal! The only criminal thing you've ever done is steal a second bun at teatime in Abbey Court!"

Mike looked a bit sheepish. "Well. The rule is one each," he said. "Unless you 'ave visitors, of course."

"Mum! Dad!" said Charlie, getting out of the back of the police car. "Why are you up at this time of night?"

"Yes!" said Vicky. "And you, Mum. What's going on?"

"We were going to come up to your flat!" said Poppy.

"What? It's eleven o' clock at night!" said Vicky.

"Yes," said Glenda. "But you remember one of Sam's birthday wishes was that all his grandparents should come for a sleepover? And have a midnight feast?"

"Um . . . yes . . ." said Charlie. "I thought that was maybe . . . just something he said . . ."

"I mean we know he's been worried sick about Grandpa Sam, so we thought we'd surprise him! For tomorrow's birthday!"

"Right . . ."

"Does a midnight feast count as tomorrow? I'd say that was today!" said Grandpa Mike.

"Oh, that's typical of you, isn't it!" said Poppy. "Always splitting hairs!"

"I just like to be precise, Poppy," said Mike.

"Annoying, I call it."

"Don't you call my husband annoying!" said Glenda.

"I'll call him what I damn well like!" said Poppy.

Charlie looked at them. "You were really coming round, right now, to have a midnight feast . . ."

"Yes, look!" said Poppy, bending down – with some difficulty – and fishing out stuff from her plastic bags.

Vicky – who'd walked over to her – looked at

the feast. Which included: a well-past-its-sell-by-date pack of digestive biscuits; a half-eaten tube of Werther's Originals; two apples not much less manky than the one still being eaten, were they only to know it, by Spock on the bank of the river; and a flask of tea, which Poppy carried with her everywhere, and which Sam didn't drink. It was so rubbish, and yet so sweet it made Vicky want to cry all over again.

"Yes . . . listen . . ." she said, not crying, but steeling herself instead. "There's no point in coming over for a midnight feast. For Sam's birthday. Because . . . Sam's gone missing. And Ruby!"

The three grandparents, for once, looked lost for words.

"Where?" said Grandpa Mike eventually.

"If we knew that, sir," said PC Middleton, "they wouldn't be missing."

Grandpa Mike looked at PC Middleton. "Well,

that's not true. You could know where they are, but until you've gone and got them from this known-about location, they are, I would say, missing."

"Oh!" said Grandma Poppy. "You are annoying! You're even being annoying with the lovely policeman now!"

"Don't you tell my husband he's being annoying!" said Glenda.

"LOOK!" said Vicky. "CAN YOU PLEASE STOP ARGUING!"

The three grandparents all looked at Vicky. Then they all looked a bit ashamed.

"I DON'T NORMALLY SHOUT AT YOU WHEN YOU'RE SHOUTING AT EACH OTHER! BUT NOW I AM! BECAUSE OUR CHILDREN ARE MISSING! AND GRANDPA SAM IS STILL MISSING. AND YOU'RE WASTING TIME SHOUTING AT EACH OTHER."

"Sorry . . ." said Grandpa Mike.

"Sorry . . ." said Grandma Poppy.

"Sorry . . ." said Grandma Glenda.

Unfortunately, they all said it at the same time, so they all started glaring at each other, as if to say: *Don't interrupt me when I'm trying to say sorry.* But then they noticed that Vicky was still staring at them, so they looked down, ashamed again.

"We're all grit-munching nerks, aren't we?" said Grandpa Mike. And they all nodded.

CHAPTER 42
BORN TO BE WILD

"OK, come on, you lot!" said a voice behind everybody. It was Carmel, coming out of Abbey Court. "Back inside . . ."

Mike, Glenda and Poppy turned round, ready to shuffle back into the sheltered accommodation. They all looked very sad.

"Hold on a minute, madam!" said PC Middleton.

"Oh no . . ." said DCI Bryant. Convinced that PC Middleton was going to say something stupid, he raised his hand to his mouth to mime the zipping motion at him. But it was dark and PC Middleton didn't see him.

"What is it, Officer?" said Carmel.

"We are looking for some missing children. The grandchildren, in fact, of these three people here. I was wondering if, rather than sending them back inside, we might be able to ask them to help."

"Help?" said Carmel.

"Yes. In a search for missing children, it's always helpful if people who know the children are around. Because they can suggest what the children might do, where they might go, based on that knowledge."

DCI Bryant stopped doing the *zip-it!* mime. He looked frankly astonished. "Er . . . yes, that is true. Very good, PC Middleton."

Carmel frowned. "Well, I see that. But how would it work? They can't come with you in your police car. There's not enough room."

PC Middleton nodded. "No. But I see you have a number of scooters parked over there?"

"I beg your pardon?"

"Yes, Middleton. What scooters?"

PC Middleton pointed to a rack of mobility scooters by the side of Abbey Court.

DCI Bryant looked back at him, incredulous. "*Those* scooters?"

But before any more could be said Grandma Poppy, Grandma Glenda and Grandpa Mike had stopped going back into the care home. Had, in fact, turned round eagerly, and were running – faster than you might think – towards the mobility scooters. By the time DCI Bryant had finished staring at PC Middleton, all three of them were mounting their chosen scooters, ready to go. Glenda had even started revving hers.

Well. It was more a whine than a rev. But she twisted that throttle like a Hell's Angel. A Hell's Angel with arthritis.

"COME ON!" she shouted. "BORN TO BE WILD!"

"In 1932 . . ." said Poppy.

"Excuse me! I'm not that old!"

"You know what?" said DCI Bryant, walking up to PC Middleton, who was watching all this, beaming happily. "I think I may actually buy you a real zip for your real mouth."

CHAPTER 43
SOME SORT OF RHYTHM

Meanwhile:

"Sam! Sam! I'm worried about Spock!"

"Yes. I think he's OK. It was quite a big bit of manky apple . . . He'll stay there nibbling on that for ages."

Ruby looked back towards the shore.

"I can't see him!"

"Don't worry, Ruby . . ."

"And how long are we going to be on here? We've rowed all the way round the island! Twice!"

That was true. The island wasn't that big: only a little bigger, really, than the size of a rich person's back garden. But it was completely covered in trees, which were very hard to see past. And so far, despite rowing very close, neither Sam nor Ruby had been able to see any sign of a star, or, for that matter, an easy place to land the skateboat.

"And . . ." said Ruby, "I've just realised something."

"What?" said Sam.

"Stars. I know they look very small up there in the sky. But they aren't, are they?"

"What?"

"Small. They're huge. Except when they die, then they shrink down to a very tiny size."

Sam frowned. "Well, maybe it's a star that's *nearly* died," he said. "Maybe that's what happens when they become a shooting star. So it's got really small."

"Actually, when they die they *do* get very small – like as small as a tennis ball – but very heavy. If a star in that state had landed on that island, it would have fallen through it by now, and ended up in Australia."

As she talked, Sam stopped rowing. They floated on the river. The sound of the water lapping against the skateboat was the only thing he could hear apart from his sister's voice. Sam thought that it was good that Ruby knew so much about the science of stars, but that the science of stars was a bit depressing.

So he kind of stopped listening. He thought about turning back, about how long it would take to row to the bank, and then, more worryingly, how long it would take to get them and *Schrodinger* back up the hill to Noam Chomsky House. He raised his broom out of the water and looked at it. The handle had a big split all the way down. He felt a little like the broom. Wet and broken and useless.

But then Ruby said something that wasn't so depressing.

"I mean, I *say* that it would have fallen through the Earth all the way to Australia. We don't know, I suppose. The thing about stars and gravity and black holes and all that physics stuff is that no one really knows what's going on. It's almost completely weird what people think might happen when you get near a star – especially one that's turned into a black hole. Some of the stuff that happens then is almost magical."

"Look!" said Sam.

"What?" said Ruby.

"A light!" said Sam. "There!"

She looked round. The skateboat was facing the middle of the island, drifting towards it. And right in the centre of the island, in what looked like the centre of the trees themselves . . . Yes, there was a light. A faint, faint, flickering light, only just visible through the leaves and branches.

Ruby frowned, and peered, to try to see better.

"Sam. I really, really don't think that's a star. It's so . . . weak!"

Sam turned to her. He put his hand on her shoulder. "Ruby. You just said that people don't really know what happens when a star dies. Maybe that's what's happening now. Maybe we will be the first people to know."

Ruby looked back at him. Then she looked at the light. It seemed to flicker in some sort of rhythm: quickly three times, then longer three times, then quickly three times again.

"Come on, then," she said, picking up her sodden broom and sticking it in the water, moving the stationary skateboat forward, towards the light, which flickered again, three quick times. "Let's go and find out!"

CHAPTER 44
MOONLIGHT MOTORCADE

Sometimes, the middle of the night is a strange time. In old books, they used to call midnight the witching hour, and they thought that was when the women with long grey hair and black cats/hats would fly around on broomsticks (just for an hour, mind).

But there is another saying: the darkest hour is just before the dawn, and some believe *that's* the time when the most weird and unusual creatures –

fairies and hobgoblins (not entirely sure what these are; goblins with small cookers, possibly) and ghosts and demons – come out to wreak their havoc.

However, presently heading down towards the river, sometime *before* these two times, there was a sight that might have been stranger than anything anyone had ever seen before. Certainly in the Bracket Wood area.

A police car was travelling down the road. Now, normally, police cars go quite fast, don't they? Especially when they have their blue flashing lights on, which this one did. But this particular police car wasn't going fast. It was going incredibly slowly. If you were walking along the pavement, at a fairly normal pace – strolling, perhaps walking the dog, and it's an old dog that limps – you would have had no problem keeping up with the police car. In fact, you'd have got to the end of the road faster than it.

The issue may have been the motorcade. This is

a word for when an important person like a prime minister or a president is driven through a city. He or she is in a car, normally a big black car, and in front and behind that car there will be police motorbikes. It looks like this:

But the motorcade presently pootling its way down Geary Road towards the river looked more like this:

To be honest, it may not have deserved the description "motorcade". After all, there wasn't a president or prime minister involved. But it's a funny idea to think of it that way.

At the front, holding up the police car – and

making DCI Bryant very much want to honk his horn, despite realising that there was no point – were Grandma Glenda and Grandpa Mike, driving very

carefully so as to stay exactly together. They both had their lights on. It wasn't a brilliantly strong light, on the mobility scooter, but that wasn't stopping them both from swaying their handlebars right and left, as if trying to sweep the road to search for the children.

At the back, also holding up the police car, as even if Glenda and Mike had not been in front of it they would have had to slow down to allow these to keep up, were Grandma Poppy, and Carmel, from Abbey Court, who had decided to come along to keep an eye on her residents.

"Well, PC Middleton," said DCI Bryant, his hand poised over the horn, still desperate to honk, "it seems to be working out very well, this idea."

"Rule number one in the Police Manual, sir. 'In a search party, always include as many people as possible who know the person or persons for whom you are searching.'"

"No, that's wrong. Rule number one is, 'Don't have stupid ideas that mean you have to drive at two miles an hour. Especially when you're in a search party, and time may be precious!'"

"Is it? Oh. Hang on . . ." Middleton said, looking in the glove compartment for the Police Manual.

"Oh gosh, not really. I'm just trying to make a point, that's all. That point being: whilst it is a good idea to bring along people who know Sam and Ruby, that good-idea-ness is somewhat cancelled out by . . ."

And it was at this point, as the motorcade – I'm still calling it that – swung slowly, very slowly, round the corner, into the road along the river, that DCI Bryant somewhat, um, lost his rag. He'd been working with PC Middleton for some time now, on a number of different cases, and had been finding it a little exhausting.

He stared at him, and shouted: ". . . THE FACT

THAT WE'RE GOING SO SLOWLY!! AND ALSO BECAUSE THE PEOPLE IN FRONT, WHO ARE SEARCHING FOR THE CHILDREN, CAN HARDLY SEE!! BECAUSE THEY'RE SO OL—!!"

"STOPPPP!! SIRRRR!!" shouted PC Middleton. DCI Bryant looked forward again, where he should have been looking rather than at PC Middleton. And for the second time that night found himself heading in a car straight towards a stock-still, stationary set of grandparents.

CHAPTER 45
CRUNCH

Part of the problem was that both Grandpa Mike and Grandma Glenda had turned their scooters round to the side in the middle of the road. So there was quite a lot more of them for the police car to hit.

Luckily, DCI Bryant – perhaps because he'd already had some practice this night – was able to slam on the brakes just in time. Again. Although not without throwing himself and PC Middleton (and Vicky and Charlie) forward in their seat belts.

"WHAT ARE THEY DOING NOWWW—"

Crunch.

Not a big crunch.

And not a crunch of the car against either Glenda's or Mike's scooters.

It was the crunch of Poppy's and Carmel's scooters, coming round the corner, against the *back* of the police car. They had been going faster than usual, because it was downhill towards the river.

"Oh great. Just great," said DCI Bryant, opening the door of the car. Charlie, Vicky and PC Middleton got out at the same time. They came round to the back of the car, where Carmel was helping Poppy up off the ground.

"Mum!" said Vicky. "Are you OK?"

"She's fine!" said Carmel.

"I'm fine!" said Poppy. "But why did you stop so suddenly?"

"It was the other two, I'm afraid," said PC Middleton.

"The ones in front. They stopped, when we got to the river."

Poppy's face set into a dark frown.

"Oh! Did they now?"

She pushed Carmel away and began marching round the police car to where Glenda and Mike were still sitting in the middle of the road on their scooters, side-on to the police car.

"Mum!" said Vicky as she strode past her. "Don't! I don't want any more shouting at each other!"

But Poppy wasn't listening. She walked up to Glenda, wagging her finger, ready to tell her off.

Glenda, however, didn't even look at her. In fact, Glenda had extended her own finger, out towards the river.

That was why she and Mike had stopped and turned their scooters round. The sweep of their lights was weak. But it had been just strong enough – only just – to see something.

Something moving close to the road, down on the banks of the river.

"LOOK!" said Glenda. *"There!"*

Everyone looked round.

"THAT'S SAM'S GUINEA PIG! ISN'T IT?"

CHAPTER 46

FLICK. FLICK. FLICK. SHINE. SHINE. SHINE. FLICK. FLICK. FLICK.

When the boat hit the island, it was no easier getting off it than it had been getting on. Sam had steered *Schrodinger* to what looked like the least muddy area, but there was a bank of rocks and stones that it just banged into again and again with the small tide. Every time he and Ruby stood up to try to jump off the skateboat, the boards would bang again on this bank of rocks and stones, making it difficult to keep their balance. Also, *Schrodinger* would then go backwards, and end up in the water again, three metres away from where they wanted it to go. Eventually Sam went:

"Oh, never mind!"

And just fell off. Deliberately.

"Sam!" screamed Ruby, putting her head over the side, and looking around for him frantically.

"It's OK!" he said, his head bobbing up in the water. "I'm already so wet it doesn't make any difference!" He swam in front of the skateboat, put one hand on it and pulled it towards the island.

In a minute, they were there. Sam held *Schrodinger* still, and Ruby got up – carefully – and walked off, on to the island. Then she turned, and held out her hand. From the water, Sam said:

"OK – hold steady."

And he reached for her hand. She held on to a branch from a nearby tree, and hauled him from the water. He stood there on the bank for a while, dripping, then shook himself in a big shiver, like a dog. Then he sneezed.

"Are you OK?" said Ruby.

"I'm fine," he said, although he sounded, to her ears, a little throaty. "Can you see the light?"

Ruby looked round behind her. It was not that friendly a sight. Just darkness and trees and scrubland. Going into the island suddenly felt like going, in the middle of the night, into the woods.

But, despite her fear, she peered deep into the trees. And . . .

"Yes! There! I think . .."

She pointed beyond the branches of the nearest tree. Sam wiped an arm across his eyes. He followed the direction of her finger. He could see it too. It was fainter and more flickery than ever. *Flick. Flick. Flick. Shine. Shine. Shine. Flick. Flick. Flick.*

It suddenly became clearer than ever to Sam what must be happening. The star *was* dying. This was its death rattle. They needed to get to it before it finally went out, if they were to reverse the magic. If they didn't, his birthday would carry on being every day, forever. And that felt, at this point, terrible, because he understood now that it would ruin his family, and indeed him, as a person, for good. Having your birthday once a year was great; having it every day, it turned out, was not.

"Hold my hand again!" he said to his sister. She nodded. Together they dived into the trees, into the darkness of the island.

CHAPTER 47
I'M A GUINEA PIG,
FOR CRYING OUT LOUD

"**Y**ou know what I wish?" said Grandma Poppy. "I wish we could ask it how it got here."

"You wish you could speak guinea pig?" said Grandma Glenda.

Poppy looked at her. She and Glenda – and Mike and Charlie and Vicky and Carmel and DCI Bryant and PC Middleton – were all standing on the bank of the river near the road, looking down at Spock, who was still nibbling on the manky apple core. Sam had been right: he *was* a guinea pig who liked to take his time over food.

"Well, now you've made it sound stupid," said Grandma Poppy. "That wish. How typical."

To be fair to Poppy, Spock was looking up at her with – in between munching – quite a strong sense of, "I could of course tell you where they are, if only you weren't so stupid as to not speak guinea pig. I, of course, understand English. I just don't speak it."

"I don't think it *is* stupid," said Vicky. She crouched down and tickled Spock on the forehead. Normally when anyone did this he ran away to hide in his cage, but this time he seemed to like it. Although possibly he just stood there accepting it, as on the riverbank there was no cage and nowhere to hide.

"Spock . . ." she said, focusing very intently on Spock's eyes (which meant, obviously, that she had to look at him first one side, then the other). "Where is Sam? Where is Ruby?"

Spock looked up at her. *Munch, munch*, he went. Also *wobble, wobble*, a bit, in his lower cheeks, like guinea pigs do.

"Oh dear," whispered DCI Bryant to PC Middleton. "I think the pressure of losing her children may have got to Mrs Green. I think she may be having some sort of breakdown."

"Sam, Spock . . . Ruby . . . Where are they?"

"Why would you say that, sir?" whispered PC Middleton.

DCI Bryant looked at him. "Because, Middleton, she's asking a *guinea pig* where her children are."

PC Middleton looked back at him. Still whispering, he retorted, "I checked the manual, sir. It definitely *doesn't* say what you said. And it definitely *does* say that the best people to aid in a search for the missing person are those who knew the missing person best."

"Yes? So? What point are you making?"

"Well, DCI Bryant, sir, as far as I understand it, Spock has lived in the same room as Sam Green. For the last year. He's been with him throughout the whole period, in fact, when Sam has been having his birthday every day. So, if anyone could be said to know the missing person well, it would be—"

"Spock? The guinea pig? That's what you're saying, is it?"

"Yes, sir."

DCI Bryant nodded. Then he reached up, and put his thumb and finger on the left side of PC Middleton's mouth.

"What are you doing, sir? If you don't mind me asking?" said PC Middleton.

DCI Bryant didn't reply. He just very slowly drew his thumb and finger across PC Middleton's mouth. While making a "ZZZZZZZZZ . . ." sound. Followed by, when his thumb and finger had reached the right side (of PC Middleton's mouth) an ". . . IP!!!" sound.

PC Middleton nodded, a little sadly.

But, actually, as he did so, someone else nodded.

"Yes?" said Vicky. "Really?"

PC Middleton and DCI Bryant looked round. Vicky and now Charlie and Carmel were crouching by Spock, who seemed finally to have finished the manky apple. Grandmas Glenda and Poppy, and Grandpa Mike, were standing by, looking down. They probably would have crouched too, if they could.

"Go on, Spock! Yes! Good boy!" they were all saying.

DCI Bryant frowned, and walked over. As did PC Middleton.

When they looked down, they saw that Spock was nodding. He was nodding his head to one side. His considerable snout and little beady eyes were bobbing, continually, to the left. It was a constant gesture. And it contained MORE than quite a strong sense of, "Over there." It said, in fact, as clear as the moon in the sky above them, "Over there." Or to be precise: "Over there is where Sam and Ruby are. On that island. What they are doing there, or why they chose to bring me, I have no idea. I'm a guinea pig, for crying out loud."

Vicky, Charlie, Grandma Poppy, Grandma Glenda, Grandpa Mike, Carmel and DCI Bryant all looked over to the island. After a short while DCI Bryant became aware that PC Middleton wasn't looking at the island.

He turned round to see that the PC was, in fact, looking at him. He – PC Middleton – had his own finger and thumb pinched on the right side of his mouth.

"UNNNNNNNNN . . . ZZZZZZIPPPPP!!" said PC Middleton, whilst drawing his finger and thumb over to the left-hand side of his mouth.

CHAPTER 48
STRONGER THAN THE NORTH POLE

The island, though small, was not easy to walk through. Especially when it was this dark. Especially when you were an eleven-year-old boy and an eight-year-old girl, and very tired, and very cold.

Even though they had only been going about twenty metres, when Ruby looked round, she could no longer see the water. It felt as if they had come into some deep and dark jungle. She held tight to her brother's hand. He suddenly stopped moving.

"Can you see the light?" said Sam, looking around. "The star?"

"No. Either it's stopped shining, or we've gone the wrong way . . ."

"OK," he said. "I think we need to do something."

"Go home?" said Ruby.

"No!" said Sam. Then he looked at her with a worried face. "Do you want to?"

"Yes. Obviously. I'm eight. I'm in the middle of an island on the river in the middle of the night," she said. But then her face hardened, and looked resolute. "But not until we find the star."

Sam smiled. "Thanks, Ruby!" He was going to hug her for a moment, but then they both realised it would just make her wetter.

"What thing should we do?" she said.

"Sorry?"

"You said we should do something? To locate the light . . . ?"

"Oh! Yes! Look!" Sam took something out of his pocket.

Ruby looked at it, screwing up her eyes in the darkness. Then it became clear. It was Grandpa Sam's battered old compass, the one that looked as if he must have used it in the First World War, even though he couldn't have done, as even Grandpa Sam wasn't that old.

The compass made Sam remember suddenly what the point of this whole secret journey was. His eyes pricked with tears at the thought.

"Yes?" said Ruby, shaking him from his trance. "What about it?" She peered down at it. The arrow was pointing to a label on the compass marked NORTH.

"Well, I just brought it because I thought it would help us find our way. But how does a compass work?"

Ruby of course knew this. "It's magnetic. It finds the magnetic field of the Earth. The North Pole is the most powerful magnetic field on the planet. So the arrow points there."

"OK. But wouldn't a star – this close – have a magnetic field that overrides the Earth one? That would be stronger than the North Pole, in other words? So when the arrow says north, what it would mean – if there was a star over there – is . . . *star.* Over there."

Ruby looked at him. "Well. Yes. But, Sam . . . I'm really not sure that light *is* a star . . ."

"You know what, Ruby? Neither am I. But do you have any better ideas?"

She looked at him. Then she looked down at the compass, which was pointing very clearly to the right.

She looked back up at him.

"No. I don't."

And off they moved, to the right.

CHAPTER 49
HELLO? HQ?

"They're on that island! I'm sure of it!" said Vicky.

"Now, now, Mrs Green. I really don't think we can be absolutely sure of that!" said DCI Bryant.

"Can you get a police boat?" said Charlie. "To take us over there?"

"What about a whole fleet?" said Grandpa Mike.

"Yes!" said Grandma Poppy. "After all, what if they've been kidnapped? And are being held hostage on that island? By terrorists?"

"Oh, can we please try and not be silly," said DCI Bryant.

"Excuse me!" said Grandma Glenda, drawing herself up to her not very full height. "No one tells my sister-in-law not to be silly!"

Everyone looked round. There had been a lot of surprising things about the events of this night so far, but this might have been the most surprising of all: Grandma Glenda standing up for Grandma Poppy. And then, to make it even more surprising, Glenda went and stood by Poppy and linked arms with her and Grandpa Mike.

"Oh blimey," sighed DCI Bryant.

Then Vicky and Charlie went over and joined the line, and so did Carmel. Even Spock came over as well. Although that might have been because he'd spotted another manky apple core next to Grandpa Mike's foot.

But DCI Bryant wasn't having any of it.

"Look!" he said. "What do you lot expect me to do?" From his chest, where it was stuck there with some Velcro, he ripped off his walkie-talkie radio and held it up in the air. "Contact Police HQ and ask them to send out a SWAT team, jet skis,

boats, frogmen, the whole lot, on the basis of a tip-off from . . . a *guinea-pig*? Really?"

At which point, PC Middleton grabbed the radio, and said:

"Good idea, sir. Hello? HQ? Did you get all that?"

CHAPTER 50
WHAT ALIENS?

As Sam and Ruby walked, tramping over branches and leaves and nettles, the compass became harder to see. It had, however, some kind of luminous tip on the needle, so if Sam held it up to his face he could make out that it was pointing, still, in the direction they were going. But it was difficult, because here, right in the middle of the island, the trees were denser than ever, and the darkness was deeper. It felt as if Sam and Ruby were not just fighting their way through the foliage, but also the dark itself.

"I can't see anything!" said Ruby.

"Hold on to my hand!" said Sam.

"I am! But what I mean is . . . I think, Sam, if there was a star we would have seen something. Or heard something."

"Heard? What noise do stars make?"

"I don't know. Some kind of . . . space noise . . . I suppose?"

And then, suddenly, they did hear something. A noise: a high-pitched whine. It rose and fell and rose again.

"What is *that*?" whispered Ruby, now very, very frightened. She looked to Sam, hoping he was not very, very frightened. Unfortunately, when he whispered back, "I don't *know* . . ." he sounded very, very, very frightened.

"Let's run away from it!" said Ruby, pulling him backwards.

"No!" said Sam, holding his ground, but tightening his hold on her hand. "Just . . . let's . . . listen for a minute." So they did. In tone, it sounded really spacey and weird, although the rise and fall had a kind of jauntiness – a jolly, almost tuneful quality.

It sounded . . . familiar.

Ruby said, "That sounds a bit like . . ."

Sam put his finger to his lips, shushing her. Then, he whispered: "Yes. But maybe that's a trick!"

"A trick?"

"By the aliens. Trying to trick our brains into hearing something nice and recognisable, which lures us into their trap!"

"Lures us into their trap? What trap? We're looking for a *star*. That's what we've been heading towards this whole time. Now you think it's a trap? And . . . what *aliens*?"

"I don't know, Ruby! I thought we would just find a bright, magical ball. I didn't think we would have to deal with . . . well, everything – Spock coming with us, and falling into the water, and the skateboat banging into the rocks, and the cold and the wet and the dark and not being able to find our way. And now I think you might be right, that it might not be a star. Maybe it was never a star! Maybe what I saw fall from the sky was . . . a UFO!"

Ruby looked at him. The whine – which now did appear to her to sound like an alien voice – grew louder. She didn't know what to think. She was a very rational child, and very interested in science. But when it came to stars, and aliens, there was lots of stuff – as she'd said herself about black holes – that science still didn't know.

However, surely, she thought, it couldn't be a star. Or a UFO. *I mean*, she thought, *not actually*.

And suddenly at that point she and Sam – in fact, what seemed the whole island – were bathed in light.

CHAPTER 51
VERY LOUD, AND THUDDING

One of the things about light is you need it to see things. But if it gets really, really bright, light *itself* is what stops you from seeing. That's called a blinding light. And that's what this light was, white and completely making it impossible to see anything. Ruby and Sam shielded their eyes, and looked up, but it seemed to be coming from the sky. Perhaps it was a star after all? Or indeed a UFO!

It was also, suddenly, getting really, really windy.

But not normal wind. The branches on the trees were bending and the leaves were flying, like . . . well, like a ship was taking off!

The noise had got much, much louder as well. Although now it wasn't just the noise of the alien whine – now it was mixed in with an engine noise, again very loud, and thudding, and repetitive. With the wind, there were so many sounds it was impossible to pick out just one to help understand what was going on!

Ruby put her arms round Sam, terrified, screaming: "You're right! It's a UFO! It's aliens!"

Sam didn't know what to say. He, too, was terrified. But he was also her big brother. So he held her close, and shouted back, over all the noise:

"Don't worry! It's going to be OK!"

Because that's what people say when they have no idea whether it is going to be or not.

Then something appeared in front of the hugging

siblings. Something which, in the blinding light, was just about visible as . . . a ladder.

"Sam Green. Ruby Green," a very big solemn voice intoned. *"Get on to the ladder. Step on to the ladder."*

CHAPTER 52
A HUMAN SHAPE

At this point, Sam, who had watched a lot of science-fiction films, thought, *Oh no. I know how this goes. We climb up the ladder. Then the aliens open the silver door in their enormous silver craft. Then we go in and there's a long, black, empty space that we float up through because there's no gravity. Then we arrive at a part of the ship that is very white and there are some strange medical-looking instruments and two operating-theatre beds. Then the aliens come in and thank us for helping them with their research . . .*

He was about to scream, "AAAAARGGGHHHHH! DON'T GO UP THE LADDER, RUBY! DON'T GO! THEY WANT TO PROBE US! THEY WANT TO . . ." when he *noticed* something about the big solemn voice.

"Don't be frightened," it was saying. "Just get on the ladder."

What he noticed about it was . . . it was what his mum had called a *Brummie* voice. It had a *Brummie* accent.

That seemed a little odd, for an alien. Obviously, Birmingham was quite a long way away. But still, in all the science-fiction films he'd seen, even when the aliens did speak English, they rarely had local accents.

"Ruby," he said to Ruby, who, he noticed, had squeezed her eyes tight shut. "Open your eyes . . ."

"I don't want to!" she said.

"No, I think it's OK."

Slowly, she did as she was told. But she still couldn't see, because the light was still very, very bright.

"Look up!" said Sam.

Ruby particularly didn't want to do that. *Up* was where the light, and the noise, and the ladder were coming from. She didn't want to look up, because it might hurt her eyes, but also because that's where the frightening aliens in their frightening ship were. Because by now even rational scientific Ruby was convinced that's what it was.

"Ruby . . ." said Sam. "Honestly. Look up."

So she did. She put her hand over her eyes and stared into the sky. At first, it looked just like a really, really bright light was up there shining down at her. Maybe it was a star, after all.

But then a shape moved across the light. A human shape, in a human uniform. And the shape shouted, "Children! It's PC Middleton! From the police! You met me at your house. Don't worry! Step on to the ladder! Climb up the ladder! And then, get on to the . . ."

"Helicopter!" said Ruby, excitedly, finally realising, through the noise, and the light, and the wind, what it was.

CHAPTER 53
DON'T SWEAR IN FRONT OF MY CHILDREN

Ruby continued to be excited as she put one foot on the ladder (which, it turned out, was a rope ladder) and reached out with her hands to pull herself on to it. But then she found she couldn't do that. She couldn't do it, because Sam had put a hand on her shoulder.

"Hold on!" he shouted up at the same time. "We came here for a reason. And we're not going back until we've found what we're looking for!"

"Er . . ." said Ruby. "When you say 'we' there . . ."

"Yes!" he said, still holding on to her. "We came here to find the star. Or . . . whatever it is that I wished on that is making my birthday happen every day! We have to reverse my wish so we can find Grandpa Sam! So we aren't going home until we've found it!"

"Yes, again, when you say 'we' there . . ."

"LOOK!" This was DCI Bryant, now also leaning out of the helicopter. PC Middleton, it turned out, was actually *flying* the helicopter. "GET ON THE LADDER! GET ON THE BLOO—!"

"DON'T SWEAR IN FRONT OF MY CHILDREN!!"

This was Vicky, who appeared from behind DCI Bryant.

Sam and Ruby looked up. They could see both their parents, looking very, very relieved in the back of the helicopter. Sitting with them was Carmel, from Abbey Court, and behind her – looking a bit silly, to be honest, in the helmets that everyone was wearing – were Grandpa Mike, Grandma Glenda and Grandma Poppy.

"Sorry . . ." said DCI Bryant. "But come on! We can't hover above this island forever!"

"Yes! Besides which, if you *don't* get on the ladder, DCI Bryant will get into terrible trouble for requesting a helicopter!!" shouted PC Middleton.

"Oh, do shut up, Middleton!"

"Have we given up saying zip it, sir?"

"No!" shouted Sam. "I want to know what the light is that's coming from this island! And you're not helping me by shining that bright light all over it. It just means I can't see anything! And that's typical of you two!"

And then, as loud as his eleven-year-old voice could get, so that you could even hear it above all the noise of the helicopter blades, he shouted:

"*You weren't any help in finding Grandpa Sam either*!"

Following which, also in a loud voice, but, weirdly,

with the tinny, metallic alien tone they had heard before, they heard someone say:

"Bracky shmizzazels! Who said my name?"

Sam looked round. Ruby looked round. DCI Bryant looked round. PC Middleton looked round. Vicky and Charlie looked round. Carmel looked round. Grandma Poppy, Grandma Glenda and Grandpa Mike looked round. The helicopter itself seemed to turn to have a look.

And standing there, holding Sam's missing-for-some-time voice-changer up to his mouth, and in his other hand, Sam's power torch, was Grandpa Sam.

CHAPTER 54
A CAMPING TRIP

Sam and Ruby dropped off the ladder and rushed over to their grandpa.

"What are *you* doing here?" shouted Sam over the sound of the helicopter blades, still swishing loudly above them.

"I'm not sure," said Grandpa Sam. "I think I—"

"Grandpa!" shouted Ruby. "Stop speaking into the voice-changer . . ."

"The what?"

"The voice-changer."

Grandpa Sam looked at Sam's voice-changer, which for some reason he was holding in his hand, and which explained the strange whiny tone to his voice. "Oh, you mean this? It's a megaphone. I need it to ward off the Biddlytongs. Banditing Biddlytongs!"

"The Biddlytongs?" said Ruby.

"Sounds just like one of his swearwords   " whispered Sam to her. But Grandpa was continuing.

"Yes. The enemy. You never know when one of them is going to creep up on you. But, you see, if I whistle into this, it changes it into a warning they understand. And they keep away!"

"Do they?" said Sam, looking around.

"Can you see them?"

Sam looked at Ruby. Ruby looked at Sam.

Then they both looked at Grandpa and shook their heads.

"Told you!" said Grandpa. Then he started

whistling into the voice-changer again.

"But why are you here at all?" asked Sam. "On this island?"

Grandpa frowned. He lowered the voice-changer. "Yes, that's what I'm finding hard to remember. I think I just wanted to get back to nature."

It was at this point that – following a sudden movement of the helicopter light, which properly illuminated him – Sam and Ruby realised that Grandpa was not actually wearing any clothes. He wasn't naked, though. He was covered in leaves and mud.

"You know," said Grandpa Sam, "I've been spending a lot of time recently . . . indoors. In this strange place. What's it called?"

"Abbey Court . . . ?"

"Yes, that's it! And you know, it's fine as far as it goes, but I just wanted to be outdoors. I always loved outdoors. I always loved camping, and swimming, and . . . just being outdoors. So I thought I'd set off for a camping trip!"

"Right . . ." said Sam.

"SAMUEL! SAMUEL!"

They looked up. It was Poppy, leaning out of the helicopter. Confusingly, she now had a real megaphone.

"Oo, hello, Poppy, my dear!" said Grandpa Sam, waving up to her. "Are you trying to ward off the Biddlytongs too?"

"WHAT?" she said.

"HE'S TALKING ABOUT THE MEGAPHONE!" shouted Sam.

"Now, for some reason," said Grandpa Sam, going back to Sam and Ruby, and ignoring the fact that his wife, who he hadn't seen for a week, was now shouting down at him from seven metres up in a helicopter, "I couldn't find all my old camping stuff so I just put together some bits and pieces as best I could . . ."

At this point he held up the voice-changer and the power torch . . .

". . . can't remember where I found these, some kind of warehouse or something – chocka with stuff it was . . ."

"I think it was my roo—" Sam began to say.

"Shh . . ." said Ruby. "Let Grandpa finish."

"SAMUEL! STOP TALKING TO THE CHILDREN! GET THEM ON THE LADDER! AND THEN YOU GET ON!"

"I THINK IT WOULD BE BETTER IF HE GOT ON THE LADDER FIRST AND THEN THE CHILDREN!"

This was Grandpa Mike. Having grabbed the megaphone off Poppy.

"I AGREE!"

Grandma Glenda. Having grabbed the megaphone off Mike.

"OH, DO YOU! YOU THINK YOU KNOW WHAT'S BEST FOR MY HUSBAND!"

Grandma Poppy, now having grabbed the megaphone back again.

"YES, YOU TELL 'EM, POPPY!! THAT'S MY GIRL!"

Grandpa Sam, on the ground, shaking his fist, through the voice-changer, which was set, now – think this was just an accident – to Mickey Mouse's voice.

"I THOUGHT YOU LOT HAD DECIDED TO ALL AGREE NICELY WITH EACH OTHER BACK AT THE RIVERBANK WHEN YOU ALL STOOD UP TO DCI BRYANT!"

This was Charlie, who had taken the megaphone from Poppy and was clearly not going to give it back to any of the grandparents any time soon. They all went quiet.

Except Grandpa Sam, who said:

"What blinking boom-schmoggling ladder, anyway?"

CHAPTER 55
WOBBLY AND WINDY AND SWAYING AND FRIGHTENING

"This one, Grandpa!" said Ruby. It had just, in fact, swung over from the police helicopter, about five metres to Grandpa Sam's left. It hung in between the three of them, shuddering with the vibrations from the helicopter above.

"Yes!" said Sam. "This one! We'll get on first, and then you, Grandpa!"

Ruby started to get on. Then she stopped.

"Sam . . ." said Ruby. He turned to her. She was at

his eye level. "You're OK to go now, even though we haven't found the star?"

Sam looked at her. He reached out, and touched her cheek. He'd never done that before.

"Grandpa *is* the star, Ruby."

"He is?"

"Yes. The light that I kept seeing on the island. From my room? It was Grandpa. Flashing my power torch." He pointed to Grandpa Sam, who was still holding the torch in his hand.

"Oh." She nodded and reached up to climb the ladder. But still didn't actually go. "Is that a bit . . . disappointing?"

Sam looked over to Grandpa Sam. In the bright light from above, they could see his kind, smiling face. Well. They could see his kind, smiling eyes, underneath a lot of mud and leaves.

"No," said Sam. "The main reason I wanted to find the star was to stop my birthday being every day so that everyone would get on with just finding Grandpa. And now we have!"

Ruby nodded again.

"RUBY!!" shouted Charlie from above. "STOP HANGING ABOUT! COME ON!"

"OK, Dad!" she shouted up. "But" – she still wasn't going – "what about your birthday happening every day, Sam? How *are* we going to stop it? If we can't find the star for you to do a new wish on it?"

Sam frowned. He didn't know the answer to this. If Grandpa was the star, he could try wishing on Grandpa . . .

But he knew that wouldn't work . . .

"I don't know, Ruby. But—"

"RUBY! PLEASE!"

"I think we'll just have to think about that later."

She nodded, for the third time, but this time raised herself upwards and climbed the rungs towards the helicopter. Sam watched as his sister got to the top.

He watched as she stretched out her arms, and as Vicky and Charlie stretched out their arms, and then watched their faces look unbelievably full of relief as those arms suddenly became full of her, of his sister.

He thought, *Well, I should go too. That looks nice. And they look — now that they've stopped hugging Ruby and she's gone to sit in the back of the helicopter with the other grandparents — like they really want me to come.*

So he started up the ladder.

It was more frightening than he'd realised. It made him think how it must have been *very* frightening for Ruby. Even though he had always been a good climber – as we know, he often went up to his own bunk bed at night without even using his hands – this ladder was *wobbly*. The whole thing was wobbly and windy and swaying and frightening.

But he was helped along by his parents and

grandparents and Carmel (and PC Middleton), who were all going:

"Come on, Sam! You can do it, Sam! You're doing so well, Sam!"

Which really did help. He looked up, rather than down, towards his parents reaching out for him . . . only one more rung to go and then he would be there . . . and then he had a thought.

He stopped climbing – he was hanging on the last section of the ladder – and looked down.

"OK, Grandpa? You ready to come up as well?"

Grandpa Sam looked at him. Then he looked up at the helicopter. Then he looked around at the island. And then he said:

"No, I think I'll stay here for a bit."

CHAPTER 56
JUST HOLD ON

"COME ON, SAM! SAM!" Vicky was shouting. "JUST ONE MORE PUSH!"

"YES, SAM, COME UP INTO THE 'COPTER!" shouted Charlie.

"YES, INTO THE 'COPTER!!" shouted various grandparents.

"SAM, REACH UP ON TO THE HELICOPTER PLATFORM IN FRONT OF YOU!" said DCI Bryant. He wasn't shouting. He now had the megaphone.

Which, frankly, was far too loud in Sam's ear at this now quite short distance.

"Grandpa's not coming!" he called back.

"WHAT?" shouted Charlie. He turned to Vicky.

"WHAT?" shouted Vicky. "DAD!! DAD!"

Down on the ground, Grandpa Sam looked up at his daughter. And waved. He *waved*.

"DON'T WAVE, DAD! WAVING IS NOT HELPFUL! GET ON THE LADDER!"

"NO, I'M ALL RIGHT!" shouted Grandpa Sam back. "OFF YOU POP!"

There was a pause. Vicky looked at Charlie. Charlie looked back at her.

"*Off you pop?*"

Glenda suddenly grabbed the megaphone off DCI Bryant, who was looking very confused. "SAMUEL! DON'T BE SO SILLY!"

Then Poppy, obviously, grabbed the megaphone off Glenda, and pointed it back at her. "DON'T TELL

MY HUSBAND NOT TO BE SO SILLY!" she said.

"Really?" said Glenda, looking at her, deadpan.

Poppy looked at her. Then nodded. Then leant out of the helicopter with the megaphone. "SAMUEL! GLENDA'S RIGHT!! DON'T BE SO SILLY!!"

"YES!" said PC Middleton. "PLEASE DO BE SENSIBLE, MR BAILEY!!"

DCI Bryant looked at PC Middleton. "You've got a second megaphone?"

"YES," said PC Middleton. Through the megaphone.

"Why didn't you say so earlier? When that lot behind us were all swapping the megaphone around? It would have made things much easier!"

"SORRY!"

"NO, THANK YOU!" shouted Grandpa Sam. "I HAVEN'T QUITE FINISHED WITH . . ." He looked around again. ". . . EVERYTHING HERE."

And then he started walking away.

Everyone on the helicopter looked confused.

"Sam!" said Vicky. "You come in, anyway! We'll come back for Grandpa!"

Sam looked at his mum, stretching her arms out. He looked at his dad, and his sister, and Carmel, and DCI Bryant and PC Middleton, and his three not-covered-in-mud-and-leaves grandparents, and he said:

"Just hold on a minute," and started to climb back down the ladder.

CHAPTER 57

TEN, NINE, EIGHT, SEVEN, SIX, FIVE, FOUR, THREE, TWO, ONE . . .

"Grandpa Sam! Grandpa Sam!" shouted Sam.

"Yes?" said Grandpa Sam, stopping.

"Do you know what day it is?"

Grandpa Sam frowned.

"You know . . . I don't think I do. I've been on this island a little while now and the days are kind of blurring into one another. A bit like they do between Christmas and New Year, you know. When you have no idea if it's . . . Monday. Or what have you . . ."

"Yes. I can tell you, though. It's the seventh of September. In fact," said Sam, looking at his watch, "it's five to midnight on the seventh of September."

"Is it? Good gracious. Doesn't time fly."

"SAM!" shouted Charlie. "COME UP! WE HAVEN'T GOT TIME FOR A LONG CONVERSATION!"

"No, that's correct, sir, we don't," said PC Middleton from the front of the cockpit.

"What are you talking about now, Middleton?"

"We may have an issue, sir," said PC Middleton, pointing at the dashboard of the helicopter.

DCI Bryant looked at where he was pointing. The fuel gauge was in the middle of the dashboard. And the needle was very much on the left of the gauge. And very much on the left, as usual, also meant very much in the red.

"Oh my gosh, Middleton! Get us out of here!"

"Well, I will, sir. Just as soon as the child actually gets on board!"

DCI Bryant turned round, fear filling up his eyes. "Mr Green! Get your boy in the helicopter! Now!"

"I'm trying!" shouted Charlie. "SAM! COME ON!"

"No, but, Grandpa," said Sam, blocking out all the shouting coming from above. "What day is it?"

"Didn't you just tell me that? Something of September?"

"Sammy! Please!" This time it was his mum. He could hear the tears, the pleading, in her voice. Sam didn't want to ignore her. In fact, he very much wanted to go up into the safety of the helicopter and fly away. It had been a very long, very cold, very wet night, and he was starting to feel not at all well.

But something impelled him to carry on. He held out one hand, away from the ladder, clutching on with the other.

"It's five minutes to midnight . . . according to the watch you gave me . . . five minutes to midnight on the seventh of September . . ."

"OH GOODNESS! WHAT IS HE DOING? WHY IS HE HAVING THIS CONVERSATION?"

This was DCI Bryant.

"I don't know," said Vicky. "I really don't know."

"But what day is it? What day is it?" Sam turned his face up to the helicopter. "What day is it, everybody?"

And then Ruby, in the helicopter, said: "I think I know what he's doing . . ."

"You do?" said Charlie.

Ruby nodded. "He's asking what day it is. What's the answer to that? What do we all think – what have we all thought for a *year* – is the answer to that?"

They all as one turned back to Sam, and said (two of them – DCI Bryant and, for some reason, Carmel, through the two megaphones):

"IT'S YOUR BIRTHDAY. OF COURSE!"

Sam nodded. And then looked to Grandpa.

Who said:

"No, it isn't. Your birthday is . . . the *eighth* of

September." He looked up at Sam, and said, "I don't remember much any more, to be honest. But I always remember that. Don't I, Sam?"

"Yes, Grandpa," said Sam, who for some reason was crying. "You always do."

"BUT IT'S HIS BIRTHDAY EVERY DAY!" shouted the people in the helicopter, as one.

Grandpa Sam looked up at them. He frowned and said through his voice-changer – although this time, for some reason, it just made his voice loud and echoey and powerful, not silly or high or like an alien's:

"DON'T BE SO STUPID! IF EVERY DAY IS YOUR SPECIAL DAY . . . THEN NO DAYS ARE SPECIAL!"

Sam looked down at his grandpa, and nodded.

But then he checked his watch, the one that used to be Grandpa Sam's. "Although . . . Grandpa!" he shouted. "Hang on! . . . Not quite now, but . . . ten, nine, eight, seven, six, five, four, three, two, one . . . *Now* it is. *Now* it's the eighth of September!"

"Oh well," said Grandpa Sam, "in that case . . ." He got on the ladder, and climbed, with apparent ease – possibly the return to nature had been healthy for him – up to Sam, and gave his grandson a kiss on the cheek. The two of them hung there in the air, on the ladder, for a moment.

". . . Happy birthday!" said Grandpa Sam.

CHAPTER 58
NOTHING

When they got back to Noam Chomsky House, at about 1am, Sam and Ruby were given a hot bath. Both of them were extremely tired, and pleased to be home.

As Sam was cleaning his teeth, though, his parents, standing outside the bathroom, were not that pleased.

"Vicky . . ." said Charlie quietly. "We need to have a strong word with him."

She nodded, but looked unsure.

"We do," continued Charlie. "He can't be allowed

to do what he did tonight! Leave the house at night without telling anyone! Take his little sister with him! Make a raft and go on the river with it! These are dangerous things! He needs to be told off!"

"Yes," said Vicky. "But firstly, it *is* his birthday . . ."

"Oh, Vicky. It's been his birthday every day for a year!"

"Yes . . . OK. But it's his *real* birthday now. And, secondly, I'm worried he's not very well. He's shivering and cold and I think everything that's happened tonight may have been too much for him . . ."

This made Charlie pause for a second.

"Well, that's as may be . . . but the fact is that I think we need to know that he's learnt his lesson. In some way."

Vicky nodded again, but still looked unsure. Sam came out of the bathroom, smiled at them and then went into his room, and started to get into bed.

"OK . . ." said Vicky. "Yes. Of course." They went into his room. Sam was sitting up in bed.

"Hey! I nearly forgot!"

He handed them a piece of paper, folded up.

"What's this?" said Vicky.

"It's my birthday list! For tomorrow! Well, today. But for when I wake up. Of course!"

Vicky and Charlie exchanged glances.

"Yes!" said Vicky, a little uncertainly. "Of course . . ."

She opened the piece of paper. Charlie leant in and looked at it too, over her shoulder. Inside, it said, on the top of page . . .

WHAT I, SAM GREEN, WOULD LIKE FOR MY 12TH BIRTHDAY:

And then, in the middle of the page underneath it, it said . . .

NOTHING.

And then underneath that:

Love, Sam.

Charlie and Vicky looked up from the piece of paper. They looked at each other. And then they both climbed up to Sam's bed to give him an enormous bundle-hug.

"Wait for me!" shouted Ruby, running in from the hall.

CHAPTER 59
BIRTHDAY TWO (THE REAL ONE)

The next day, the eighth of September, that is exactly what happened. Nothing. Sam was woken by his parents looking down at him. It felt as if they'd only just finished bundle-hugging him. But Sam had a sense that some time had passed. So he said, sleepily,

"Hey. What time is it . . . ?"

"It's nearly midnight . . ." said Vicky quietly.

"Oh, OK." Then Sam frowned. "Wait a minute.

It was one o'clock when we got home yesterday morning . . . so how can it be midnight . . . ?"

"Because, Sam," said Charlie, "you slept. All day.
"You slept . . . all through your birthday."

Sam frowned again. He frowned, firstly, because it's always hard to believe you've slept for a long time when you have. It takes a little while to adjust. But he frowned, secondly, because he realised . . . that this was a brilliant way to spend his birthday. He loved sleeping, and he loved staying in bed, so he sort of wished he'd thought of it before, as a way of spending one of his many birthdays.

But, actually, it *was* the best way to spend his real birthday. Because he'd said that he wanted nothing. And that included doing . . . nothing. So being allowed to spend all day asleep in bed, sleeping off his exhausting year of birthdays, was perfect. Having thought all this through, his frown vanished. But then it came back again.

"OK . . . so why are you waking me up?"

"You can go back to sleep. But we wanted to give you something," said Charlie.

It was then that Sam realised that his dad was holding a box.

"Dad . . ." he whispered. "I said. No presents. Remember?"

"Yes," said Vicky. "We remember. But we wanted to do something for you on your birthday. Even if it wasn't buying you a present."

"So . . ." said Charlie, "we went back to the river. We spent a long time down there. And eventually we found what we wanted to give you today. Two things, in fact."

Vicky bent down, and picked up something, and held it up to him, over his bed.

"This . . ."

It was his skateboard. Just one of them. The other three had clearly gone, somewhere under the river.

But the original one, with its flexiboard, and trucks, and red wheels, here it was! It was a bit scratched and battered, but if anything that just made it look cooler.

"Wow! Brilliant, Mum! Thanks!"

"And . . ." said his dad, holding out the box.

Sam's frown deepened. He sat up, reached over and lifted the lid.

Well, that's not true. He was *about* to lift the lid, when a tiny, furry snout poked out of the box, followed by some whiskers and, finally, some eyes.

"Spock!" shouted Sam, lifting the guinea pig out of the box and up in the air, with both hands.

And Spock looked down at him with quite a strong sense of, "Well, I *was* thinking of going on that raft all the way to the Andes, which is, in fact, where I come from, but having said that I'm actually quite pleased to see you too!"

CHAPTER 60
CASE SUCCESSFULLY CLOSED

And then Sam went back to sleep. Because he was still tired. And because now, for him, the really important day was not the eighth of September, even though that was a day he used to look forward to for so long. The *really* important day was the ninth of September. He wanted to go to sleep before midnight on the eighth, and then wake up on the morning of the ninth to see if what he hoped was indeed true.

*

Sam woke to the sound of the birds singing at around 7.30am. He lay in bed. Which might seem odd, since he'd been in bed for so long. He wasn't tired. He felt much, much better. The long sleep had done him good, and any poorliness he'd had from the night getting to the island had vanished. So why didn't he get up?

Because he was waiting for a knock on the door. That little, gentle knock that meant his mum was behind it holding a tray. With a special birthday breakfast on it.

He was waiting for that knock . . . really, really hoping it wasn't coming. He wasn't sure how long you have to wait for something that you're hoping isn't going to come. Before you know it isn't.

But then he realised that he'd been thinking about it for so long that the answer had arrived:

his mum was definitely not going to be doing that knock on the door.

No, on the ninth of September, Vicky did not come into Sam's bedroom with a special birthday breakfast-in-bed tray. And neither were there any presents for Sam, or cakes, or singing of "Happy Birthday"; no trips to the cinema, or to Go Ape, or to an indoor climbing rock; and there was no party. Unless you call Grandpa Mike, Grandma Glenda, Grandma Poppy and Grandpa Sam sitting around, drinking tea and watching telly, a party. In which case, you need to get out more.

Grandpa Sam, in fact, had spent the previous day in hospital, being checked out by doctors following his time on the island. But, apart from a bit of a cold, he turned out to be fine. Well, not fine – as perhaps you will have realised, Grandpa Sam had a thing called dementia, which old people sometimes get – but physically, the doctors explained, he was remarkably fit for a man of his age. So they let him go.

Carmel had come round to Noam Chomsky House as well, to keep an eye on him, and make sure he didn't go wandering off again. While everyone was there, DCI Bryant and PC Middleton turned up. It was procedure, they said, to come round to check that all was OK now, and wrap up the case.

"It appears . . ." said DCI Bryant to the entire family and Carmel, "that Mr Bailey here . . . by which I mean Grandpa Sam . . . had managed to leave Abbey Court with a bag of things purloined from your son, including a voice-changer and a super-bright torch . . . Will you be wanting to file charges, by the way?"

This was directed to Sam. Sam looked at Grandpa Sam, who was smiling at him.

"Er . . . no, DCI Bryant."

DCI Bryant made a face. "Well . . . it's up to you."

"Did he . . ." said Charlie, "swim there? To the island?"

"It appears so."

"He used to swim for the county," said Poppy proudly, linking her arm with Grandpa Sam's. "That's when I first remember falling in love with him, seeing him at our local pool."

"Did he keep his trunks on that time?" said Glenda slyly.

Poppy shot a cross glance at her, but DCI Bryant continued:

"Yes, we'll be filing a report. Case successfully closed. The children found, and of course, Samuel Bailey, also found. Well done, Middleton."

"Thank you, sir. For what?" said PC Middleton.

"For finding the children. Of course. And Mr Bailey. I shall – in my report – be commending both of us."

"I see, sir. Will you be mentioning, though, that

it was, in fact, the children – Sam and Ruby – who actually found Mr Bailey?"

"Middleton . . ." said DCI Bryant.

"Moreover," said PC Middleton, "that it was actually Spock the guinea pig who found – or at least directed us towards – the whereabouts of the children?"

"MIDDLETON . . ."

DCI Bryant started to do the zip gesture with his mouth towards PC Middleton. But Sam said:

"DCI Bryant! You're, um . . . flying low . . ."

Everyone looked down. At DCI Bryant's zip. Which was indeed . . . low. DCI Bryant went very red. But not before PC Middleton could go:

"Zip it! . . . Sir."

CHAPTER 61
HE'S ALWAYS GOING TO BE HERE

A few other things happened that day. Sam told his mum that he thought it might be a good idea if they took all his presents and sold them on the internet: which if you remember is what Vicky did as her job.

"Are you sure?" said Vicky.

"Yes. Please. I've got no room in my room! And also . . . I know this year has been hard . . . for you and Dad . . . for money, I mean . . ."

"Well . . . yes . . . but . . . don't you want to keep anything?"

Sam thought for a moment. "OK. Yes. The binocuscope."

Vicky nodded.

"You're thinking you won't be able to sell that anyway, aren't you? Because it's basically two broken things stuck together . . ."

"No . . ." said his mum, smiling. "OK, yes. Anything else? What about your skateboard . . .?"

Sam frowned. He did like the skateboard very much. But he'd had a thought about that.

"I will hold on to that too. For a little while . . ." Then, Sam lowered his voice, and said, "But we have to have some money, because Ruby, she wants . . ."

"Hello, everyone!" said Charlie, coming through the door. "Guess where me and Ruby have just been?"

There was a second when Sam and Vicky and all the grandparents looked at them with simply no idea. All they could tell was that Charlie was smiling and Ruby was really, really smiling (and standing with her hands behind her back). But then from behind Ruby's back they heard a tiny, high meow. And then another one. So – basing his conclusion mainly on the tiny, high meows – Sam said:

"The pet shop?"

Ruby and Charlie glanced at each other, smiling even more. Then Ruby brought her hands round from behind her back, and falling floppily from her gentle grip was a beautiful, fluffy, long-haired ginger kitten.

"Oh my goodness, Ruby, he's gorgeous!" said Vicky, rushing over to stroke him. All the grandparents came over as well, pushing each other to try to get their hands near the cat.

"He's stonkblonkingly lovely!" said Grandpa Sam.

"He is," said Sam, smiling. "What's his name?"

"What do you think?" said Ruby.

"Hang on . . ." Sam screwed up his face, trying to remember. "What was it . . . Scrowdingdong?"

"Schrodinger! Yes! That's his name!"

"Does that mean he's going to be here and not here?" said Sam.

"No!" said Ruby, cuddling the sweet tiny face to her face. "He's *always* going to be here. Actually!"

Charlie and Vicky looked on, open-mouthed, wondering just when their children – *both* their children – had become so clever.

CHAPTER 62
ONCE A WEEK, AT NIGHT

Later in the day, Sam told his parents that he wanted to go and check if his skateboard was still working. So they let him out to play by himself. He took the lift down, pressing G, and trying, as ever, not to breathe the smell of wee. This may be a magic story in some ways, but that *hadn't* changed.

He rode the board out of Noam Chomsky House, and over to the bowl, under the block. He was, he could tell, a better skateboarder now, following his experience with the skateboat. It felt so much easier to ride, after all, than that had. He kicked off and rode the bowl, round the sides, up and down, flipping and jumping, like crazy.

But he wasn't just skateboarding. He was doing two things. One of them was waiting. He kept going for ages, upping his trick level, getting faster and faster, until dusk started to fall.

Then he heard a voice.

"Hello!" said Zada.

"Hello!" said Sam, skating up to meet her on the edge of the bowl. "I was waiting for you!"

"Oh, right," said Zada. "You OK?"

"Yeah," said Sam.

"Where's the biggie?" said Zada, pointing at Sam's normal board. It seemed that, over time, she had started to speak a bit more like an English kid speaks.

Sam shook his head.

"That's a pity. It was sick," she said.

"Yeah."

"But that board is cool too."

"Thanks," said Sam. Then he said, "Would you like it?"

Zada frowned. "What?"

"Well . . . I just thought – you're such a brilliant skateboarder. And I can see your board . . . I mean it looks cool, but it's starting to fall apart . . . a bit . . ."

Sam held it out for her: his flexiboard, with its shiny trucks and red wheels.

Zada looked at him. "But . . . why?"

Sam smiled. "To say thank you."

Zada nodded. "That's so nice of you. I . . ."

"Don't say no. I really want you to have it."

Zada looked up from the board at Sam. It was clearly true. But at the same time Sam could tell she wasn't sure. He remembered what she'd said about her dad making her old one. And how when he'd asked about her dad, she'd said nothing, and just twirled its wheels.

"Well . . ." she said, and took it, putting her old one down. It wobbled slightly on the ground, not sitting there completely straight. "Maybe. But what will you do, for a board . . . ?"

Sam thought about it for a minute. Then he picked up Zada's old board. "Do you mind if I have this? I think I might be able to fix it up. I'm good at making and building stuff."

Zada looked at him, and then at her board, which her dad had made for her once, in another country, long ago. "Yes. Please. That would be very nice."

For a second, Sam thought she might be going to cry. He wouldn't have quite known what to do if she had.

Luckily, instead, she said:

"Do you want to come skating now?"

"No," said Sam. "I have to go back in to see my

family. But maybe we could meet up here and work out some moves? Like once a week, at night?"

"Sure," said Zada. Then she put what had been Sam's board on the ground, flipped up the nose and off she went – down into the bowl, weaving and bobbing and spinning and making that grim concrete place seem like a sunlit sea.

Sam watched, and smiled again. And, as he had been doing for a while, he said to his board, very happily, goodbye.

CHAPTER 63
DASH DASH DASH. DOT DOT DOT. DASH DASH DASH.

B ut even though nothing birthday-ish happened to him that day – only to Ruby – Sam was still not entirely, *entirely* sure that the birthday magic was over. When the grandparents left, later that night, Sam made sure to say a proper goodbye to Grandpa Sam.

"Are you OK, Grandpa? Are you all right to go back to Abbey Court now?"

"Don't worry," said Carmel. "I'll make sure he

gets more time in the garden. I think that's what he needs: to be outside. Isn't that right, Sam?"

"That is right, Carmel," said Grandpa Sam. "Back to naughty nature. As I like to say."

"You do, Sam. You do . . ."

"Otherwise I might be off! Into the wollocking wild!" he said.

"Yes," said Carmel. "You might be. And then what would we do?"

"I'd have to send out a distress signal! With a telegraph. Or a radio! SOS! SOS! Only bit of Morse code you need to know, that."

"What's that, Sam?" asked Carmel.

"Dash dash dash. Dot dot dot. Dash dash dash. Never forget that. Scout's honour!"

"Or . . ." said Sam – the boy – "You could do that with a torch, couldn't you, Grandpa?" He was thinking of the light on the island, and its peculiar rhythm. "Three short flashes . . ."

"Three long flashes, and three short flashes! Yes! I've taught you well."

"Yes, all right, Samuel," said Grandma Glenda. "No need to rub it in. We know you think you're Sam's favourite!"

"I do *not* think that."

"Oh, don't you?" said Grandpa Mike.

"No!" said Grandpa Sam. "I *know* I'm his favourite!"

Following which, all hell broke loose. Within seconds, they were all shouting and screaming as usual.

Sam watched as his grandparents continued to shout and scream at each other for ages, with no one telling them to stop. And he smiled. Because he knew then that no one was going to think it was his birthday again until the next eighth of September.

Which made it a very, very happy ninth of September.

CODA

About a year later – in fact, on Sam's thirteenth birthday – a strange sight was reported on some news websites from the seas around an island called Tortuga, off the coast of Peru.

A rudimentary boat – or a raft – was reported as having been washed up on this island. And then, a few days later, the same boat-raft could be seen sailing off from land . . . covered in guinea pigs.

Over a hundred of these guinea pigs, native to the Andes, were seen, all facing forward, all with very intent expressions on their faces, as if they all knew where they wanted to go. Almost as if they were keen to see one of their own, to whom they were journeying out to meet. Early reports even suggested that the boat-raft was being paddled by the guinea pigs with their tiny feet, and was heading – although many disputed that this could possibly be the case – in the direction of the UK.

But then, after the initial reports, the boat seemed to evade the sight of humans who wanted to explain this phenomenon and follow its path. The boat appeared, in fact, to be both there and not there.

But I imagine it will turn up at some point.

Acknowledgements

I'd like to thank, for their invaluable help making this book happen: as always, my illustrator, the genius Jim Field; everyone at HarperCollins, including Samantha Stewart, Geraldine Stroud, Charlie Redmayne, Jo Hardacre, Kate Clarke, Elorine Grant, and particularly Ann-Janine Murtagh and Nick Lake, who continue to be my twin lode stars of children's fiction; my literary agent and general astonishing force for good, Georgia Garrett; Julien Matthews and Grace Rodgers at Avalon; audio-book whisperer (and exhaustive writer-down-of-extra-mistakes-spotted-during-the-read) Tanya Hougham; and as ever, my family, although having said that Ezra promised to read the proof but never did.

Discover more
Baddiel Blockbusters!

First, don't miss David Baddiel's hilarious
AniMalcolm, out now in paperback.

Malcolm doesn't like animals . . . which is a problem because his family love them. Their house is full of pets. What the house is NOT full of is stuff Malcolm likes. Such as the laptop he wanted for his birthday.

The only bright spot on the horizon is the Year Six school trip, which Malcolm never thought his parents would pay for. And yet there he is, when we join the story, on the coach . . .

Turn the page for an extract...

The Bracket Wood Primary School coach was having trouble getting down the hill.

This might seem unusual: you would expect most vehicles as old and creaky as the Bracket Wood Primary School coach to have trouble getting *up* this particular hill, a hill in the middle of the countryside renowned for its steepness. And of course it *had* done when it had driven up the other side – the climb had taken an hour and a half, and at one point most of

Year Six had started
screaming, "It's going to
roll backwards! It's going to roll
backwards!" and cowering under their seats.

But once over the top, even the rustiest
rustbucket should be able just to glide all the way
down. As it was, though, it seemed less to glide
than to… cough. And splutter.

None of this was helped by the weather, which,
though it was spring, was rainy and foggy.

Malcolm sighed, closed his eyes and tried to
rest his forehead on the shuddering window. Up

ahead he could see a flock of sheep running away from them as the coach belched its way forward. The vehicle finally managed to gain some speed and pass the sheep, but Malcolm noticed that they carried on running, even though there was nothing behind them any more. In fact, that they were now basically chasing the bus they were supposed to be running away from.

Some boys at the back – a boy called Barry, and his friends Lukas, Jake and Taj – turned round to point at the sheep, running away from nothing, and laughed. But Malcolm just felt annoyed at the stupid stupidity of the stupid sheep.

Eventually they made it to the bottom of the hill, and their destination.

"We're here!" said their teacher, Mr Barrington, peering out of the front window. "I think…"

He said "I think" partly because his eyesight was not of the best – he had very, very thick glasses – and partly because the sign he was looking at was obscured by mist.

But *as* he said "I think", the mist cleared to reveal the words:

ORWELL FARM

"Yes, this is definitely the place," he said. "Drive on, driver, quick-smart! Let's waste no more time getting the children *out* of this bus, *on to* the farm, and starting to look after all the animals!"

"Hooray!!" went all the children.

Well, all except one.

Oh no. A farm.

But over the next few days, Malcolm changes. He learns a lot about animals. More, in many ways, than he would like. It makes him think differently. And speak differently. And eat differently. And, um, smell differently. But will he end up the same as before?

Because sometimes the hardest thing to become is . . . yourself.

Find out what happens next in: